The Great Eye

· · · Phyllis Shalant

The Great Eye

Dutton Children's Books
New York

Library of Congress Cataloging-in-Publication Data

Shalant, Phyllis.
The great eye / by Phyllis Shalant.—1st ed.   p.   cm.
Summary: Writing poetry on a computer and working with a labrador
retriever guide-dog candidate help twelve-year-old Lucy deal with
feelings of loss during her parents' separation.
ISBN 0-525-45695-3
[1. Dogs—Fiction.   2. Guide dogs—Fiction.   3. Divorce—Fiction.
4. Poetry—Fiction.   5. Computers—Fiction.]   I. Title.
PZ7.S52787Gr   1996
[Fic]—dc20   96-24559   CIP   AC

Published in the United States by Dutton Children's Books,
a division of Penguin Books USA Inc.
375 Hudson Street, New York, New York 10014
Printed in USA
First Edition
2 4 6 8 10 9 7 5 3 1

For my mother, Anne Fisher Jushpy Scherwin

Acknowledgments

To the poet, Joan Pardes, special thanks for showing me the fine points. And to Guiding Eyes for the Blind in Yorktown Heights, New York, my gratitude for all that you taught me about raising dogs—especially those with a special mission—and for what you do for all of us.

A poem . . . begins as a lump in the throat,
a sense of wrong, a homesickness, a lovesickness.
It finds the thought and the thought finds the words.

Robert Frost

The Great Eye

1

~~I drink the summer blue air~~

~~I swallow the summer sky~~

~~I bite the blue air of summer~~

~~I chew the blue~~

~~I gulp the sky blue air of summer~~

I gulp the azure air of summer
till I fall down dizzy, laughing, wondering
Is this what it's like to be drunk?

Lucy Rising repeated the verse in her head six times as
she hurried home. It was the way she always memorized lines she couldn't copy down right away. The
word *azure* wasn't really her own. She'd stolen it from
Emily Dickinson, who'd used it in a poem describing a
perfect afternoon. But azure was exactly how Lucy felt
today. Not because it was the last day of seventh grade,
or the weather was completely gorgeous, but because
her sister, Anna, was coming home from college that
night.

Although Lucy had finished her sister's homecoming poem a week ago, she hadn't tacked it up on the door to Anna's room yet. She'd been waiting to find just the right picture to go with it. Before Anna went away, the two of them had often spent entire days making cards, posters, and little books for birthdays, anniversaries— every holiday or happening they could think of to commemorate. One of Lucy's favorites was the poster they'd given their father after he got a speeding ticket on the way to see a women's tennis exhibition. On a large sheet of posterboard, Lucy had written a poem titled "Experience."

EXPERIENCE
We've heard it said, Dad,
"Experience is the greatest teacher"
But after feeling—
the palm of your hand at our backs
when we were wobbling down the block
on our new two-wheelers; taking turns
riding on your shoulders through the zoo
while you explained why the lion roared,
why the monkey pooped in his cage, and why
we really should try walking more

After feeling—
your arms around our shoulders
    under the night sky

while you pointed out the Big Dipper,
    the North Star
and those little purple people
And giggling nervously in the backseat
while you raced that policeman
just to teach us the consequences,
Dad, we know
experience can't hold a candle to you
and we promise, never, ever to speed

Under Lucy's poem, Anna had drawn a cartoon showing the two of them peering out of the car while their
father was talking to a policeman. The cop's eyebrows
looked like two fuzzy horseshoes, and his hat was pop-
ping off his head in surprise, or maybe frustration. Underneath the drawing, Anna had written the caption:
"Couldn't you just think of it as driver education, Officer?"

Mr. Rising had hung the poster over the desk in
what used to be Lucy's parents' bedroom. Six months
ago, during Christmas vacation, he'd moved out, taking
it with him. For a while, Lucy used to go into the room
and run her hand across the empty space on the wall.
Then her mother put a calendar there.

By the time Lucy got home, she'd decided to tack
up Anna's homecoming poem without a picture. Instead, she intended to glue sticks of Big Red gum—
their favorite—around the edges of the paper like a
frame. As she plopped her book bag down on a chair in

the kitchen, she noticed the light on the answering machine blinking. She poured herself some orange juice and pressed PLAY.

"Lucy, this is Brenda Botts," a voice said. "I may have a dog for you. Please call me at Guiding Friends of the Blind as soon as possible."

Lucy's heart flip-flopped like a freshly caught fish on a dock. She'd wanted a dog for as long as she could remember. But always, her parents had countered her pleas with the same unanswerable question. "We both work. You go to school. Who will take care of it?" Then, after Christmas, her mother had suggested Guiding Friends. She'd told Lucy she thought a puppy would be good company and that doing a community service like raising a guide dog would be a valuable experience.

Neither of which was the real reason for her mother's change of heart, Lucy was certain. The truth was, her mother felt sorry for her. Lucy had wanted to snap that she didn't need company or sympathy. But she'd only said, "Thanks Mom, I'd love to."

"A dog has just become available, and I thought he might be a good choice for you, Lucy," Brenda Botts was explaining. "He's an older pup, a year-old black Labrador retriever, whose raiser just moved out of the area. He's not quite ready for our professional program yet, so I thought you might be willing to keep him this summer so he can finish his obedience classes. It would be a good introduction to dog-raising, and by the time he gets promoted, we should have a younger puppy ready for you."

The telephone receiver suddenly felt like a weight in Lucy's hand, a mini-dumbbell like the one at the back of her mother's closet. She closed her eyes and tried to picture a year-old Lab. The dog she saw was not little and cuddly. It was big and strange and used. A reject. She considered saying that she preferred to wait for another dog, but something wouldn't let her. What if this dog felt abandoned? What if it woke up each morning with the sense that something was missing and felt like going back to sleep when it remembered what that something was?

"What's the dog's name?" She wanted to ask if it seemed depressed, but she was afraid that would sound dumb.

"His name is Hobart. Can someone drive you over here to pick him up tomorrow morning, say around ten?"

"Yes, I think so."

"Good. I'll see you then."

Lucy went back to the table and pasted the Big Red sticks around the edges of her poem. Maybe Anna would take her to pick up the dog. She loved driving with her sister. Even though Anna had gotten her license nearly two years ago, being alone with her in the car still gave Lucy a giddy, exhilarating feeling, like they were breaking the rules.

She hadn't felt that way in the beginning, though. Especially not on the day Anna turned sixteen and their father had come home early from work to take Anna for her first driving lesson. Lucy had demanded to come along. It was one of the few times she remembered her father refusing her anything. "Your turn will come," he'd promised. When she'd kept on whining and complaining, he'd added, "Jealousy is unbecoming, Lucy. It turns your skin the color of artichokes."

After they'd driven away, Lucy had sat on the front steps and stared at her hands. She'd thought she could actually detect a dull greenish tinge starting around her fingernails.

In three years and three months, Lucy would be able to get her driving permit. Who would teach her? Her mother? Anna? If she reminded her father of his promise, would he come home to keep it? He'd taught Anna to drive his car because it was a stick shift. "That way you'll be able to handle anything," he'd explained. But Lucy's mother drove an automatic. How could Lucy learn to handle anything if an automatic was the only car they had?

She pasted on the last stick of gum and went to hang the poem on Anna's door.

ABSENCE MAKES THE HEART GROW
While you were gone
I baked our special Surprise Bars
But even though I didn't burn them,
they weren't so surprising.

I polished my toenails 'Scarlet Fever'
with the bottle you left in the bathroom,
but I botched up the pinkies and dripped on the
    carpet
and the polish remover left a trail of white spots.

On Sundays, I ate both halves of our bagel
and didn't have to share the comics—
only they weren't so funny.

I rented *East of Eden*
and found you were right—
James Dean was totally gorgeous.

I wore your nightgown, slept in your bed,
borrowed your dreams.
They didn't fit.

Lucy stepped back and gazed at the type, which was black and even, not like the fancy hand-lettering Anna used to do with her colored pens and swirly script. Yet she'd never thought of her computer as a lifeless thing. From the first time she'd turned it on, the bright blue screen had blinked wide open like a giant, understanding eye. So she'd named it The Great Eye. It was a Christmas gift from her father. A surprise. He'd said he hoped it would give her wings. A week later, he was gone.

From downstairs, Lucy heard her mother singing "Feelin' Groovy." She could usually gauge her mother's mood by her songs, but it didn't take a detective to figure out she would be happy today.

"Oh, sweetie, I am so glad school's out," Mrs. Rising said when Lucy entered the kitchen. "I am seriously ready for a change!"

"Well, working as a counselor for a bunch of little monsters will be different from being a school librarian, Mom. A lot different. After the first day, you'll probably wish you were staying home all summer like you used to."

"They're not little monsters, they're campers. With special problems. And I still wish you would have let me enroll you in a camp, or at least in tennis or swim lessons. You know, there's still time. It's only the last week of June. I'm sure we can find something you'd like to do."

Lucy fought the rise that was swelling in her throat. She didn't want to start the vacation by arguing with her mother. "I already told you I have something I like to do. I'm going to write poetry and spend time with Anna. And Calvin! I hardly get to see him now that he's changed schools."

"But you need new experiences, too. It's important to get on with your life."

Lucy stopped listening. Maybe new experiences were what her mother needed, but they weren't what she needed. She didn't want to change her life. She'd had enough changes to last forever. "I hope you bought dog food," she said, peering into the grocery bag Mrs. Rising had set on the counter.

"Oh! Did Guiding Friends call you about a puppy?"

"Sort of. They want me to take a one-year-old Lab for a couple of months. He needs a home until he's ready for their training program."

Mrs. Rising screwed up her face so her nose and lips twisted off to the left. Lucy knew she was thinking up reasons why they should be pleased. Her mother was a great rationalizer. On the day Lucy's father left, she'd gone into her room and locked the door for several hours. When she came out again, she was dragging a laundry basket behind her. Lucy followed her to the driveway and watched her dump the contents into a garbage can. "At least I won't have to wash his stinking tennis socks!" her mother had announced. The skin around her eyes had looked pink and swollen, like worms after a spring rain.

One early spring day when Lucy was nine, she'd gone Rollerblading. But the streets were still cracked and buckled from the hard winter, and she'd tripped and fallen on some broken glass. At the emergency room, the doctor had dug into her bloodied flesh with a tweezer, picking out the slivers one by one. The pain had been so sharp, she hadn't been able to stop screaming. But now she tried to remember it. To feel it even. She welcomed anything strong enough to block out the memory of her mother's wormy eyes.

"At least a year-old dog will be housebroken," Mrs. Rising said, finally. "And he'll sleep through the night."

"But I wanted something cuddly and lovable."

"You're bigger than I am and I still love you." Mrs. Rising stood on her toes so she could kiss Lucy's cheek. At five-foot-five, Lucy was a full three inches taller than her mother. She had her father's long legs, as well as his dark hair. It was Anna who took after Mrs. Rising, blonde and petite. Except Anna was the one who'd gotten Mr. Rising's blue eyes—a fact which had always seemed unfair to Lucy.

Lucy gave her mother a quick bear hug and kissed her on top of the head just to show off. "We have to pick the dog up at Guiding Friends tomorrow at ten. What's for dinner?"

"Pasta and pesto, Anna's favorite." Mrs. Rising looked up at the clock on the wall. "She should be here soon." Then, as if she just remembered, she added, "You got a letter. I left it on the dining-room table."

Lucy knew right then it had to be from her father. Otherwise, her mother would have carried it all the way into the kitchen. She headed out to get it, careful not to run.

Sure enough, a wide-eyed koala stared at her from the envelope. She'd learned to recognize her father's stamps by the weird animals on them—creatures you could only find in Australia, like the duckbill platypus, the wombat, and the wallaby. And now, Mr. Rising himself.

Lucy pressed the letter to her nose and breathed in. The scent of cigarettes and shaving soap was unmistakable. It was how her father smelled and how their bathroom had smelled, too, for a long time after he'd moved out.

Actually, her father wasn't supposed to have smoked in the house. Her mother wouldn't allow it. She'd quoted study after study clearly showing that second-hand smoke was especially bad for children. Finally, Lucy's father had given in. Not that he'd given up the habit, but he didn't smoke at home anymore—except for one cigarette in the bathroom, first thing in the morning. Lucy thought her mother had to be aware of this transgression, even though she'd pretended otherwise. She had even thought her mother secretly liked the smell as much as she did. But once spring arrived, her mother had kept the window open until the smell was nearly gone.

Lucy turned the envelope over and checked the return address. Her father was still staying at the home of his client, S. Markham, at 122 Bellingham Road in Brisbane. When she turned it back, she realized he'd addressed the envelope to Lucy Storm Rising. Her real name was Lucy Rose Rising. He was letting her know he'd received the school magazine which had published her poem, "Storm Queen."

Suddenly, she wished she'd never sent the poem to him. She wished she'd never shown it to her English teacher, Mr. Frye. She wished she'd never written it at all.

Yet she knew if she took out her copy of the magazine and flipped to the poem, she would feel a thrill that swelled and crashed against her insides like the waves at the shore. It still surprised Lucy that her poem had made it into *Freestyle*. Usually, *Freestyle* was reserved for the work of the older kids. Of course, if Mr. Frye hadn't submitted it for her, it never would have happened. But when it came to poetry, Mr. Frye was a man with a mission.

"When you write a poem, you are like a magician,

because poetry can turn a piece of paper into anything you choose," he'd told the class. "If you are happy, your poem can be fireworks on a summer night or a fast dance. If you are sad, your poem can be a butterfly with one wing or a blind jump into a canyon. If you're angry, your poem can be a scalding kettle or a broken bottle."

Lucy had felt like tearing paper from her notebook and writing a poem right there and then. But she'd kept the feeling in until she got home. Then she wrote "Storm Queen."

I am Storm Queen
My legs a swirling spray of icy mist
My arms two bolts of current
Spiky fingers sparking earth
My body a deep, dark vacuum sucking
Earth, Air, Fire, Water
My throat wailing winds cold and raw
My eyes weeping rain that makes earth sleep
My heart pumping destruction
Across the slumbering planet

She turned it in for an assignment about nature symbolism in poetry. The next day, Mr. Frye asked her to stay a minute after class. "Lucy, this is good. Powerful and angry," he said, holding "Storm Queen" in his hand. "You must have been having a bad day when you wrote it."

A bad day, a bad week, a bad month, Lucy thought. Which was exactly how long her father had been gone. A month. She'd never stood so close to Mr. Frye before. She could tell he used the same shaving soap as her father. But the sharp, forbidden scent of tobacco was missing. The lack was like forgetting to add the quarter teaspoon of salt when you baked chocolate chip cookies. Flat. Disappointing.

Mr. Frye had cleared his throat. "Do you want to talk about it?"

"I'm fine now. Really." Lucy suddenly had had the embarrassing sense that she'd taken her clothes off in public—even worse in a way, because now Mr. Frye could see the stuff under her skin.

In the beginning, her mother hadn't wanted anyone to know what had happened. "Um, Lu? Don't—don't say anything to anyone about this," she'd stammered the morning after Christmas vacation, just before Lucy left for school. "If he changes his mind and comes back, we can forget about it. Kind of like a bad dream, right?"

"Right." Lucy had felt her mother's shame glowing like charcoals in her own chest, sending heat to every corner of her body. They belonged to that other category now. The families who'd been divided or deserted. Or both.

"Your dad's unpredictable, you know that, Lu. He could change his mind and be back here in time for lunch."

Had her mother actually thought the pilot would make a U-turn around the nearest cloud if her father asked him to?

"Lucy? Would you mind if I submitted your poem to *Freestyle*?" Mr. Frye had asked.

Mind? Lucy had been ecstatic. She had wondered how a person could be on the verge of crying one minute and laughing the next.

Dear Lulu:

By the time you receive this, I guess school will be over. What are you going to do this summer? I hope you will take the opportunity to experience lots of new things. That's what I'm doing. Last weekend I went diving along the Great Barrier Reef and saw dozens of creatures I'd never even dreamed existed. I brought up some conches, which my friend fixed for dinner (I didn't admit they tasted like rubber bands).

Have you written any new poems lately? I have been reading poems and stories by the Australian writer Henry Lawson. His work is all about life in the bush (which means the countryside) in the 1890s. I haven't seen much of the bush yet, but I plan to soon.

Lucy, I was so grateful to receive the copy of your school magazine with your poem in it. I wish you would have included a note, too, but it's a beginning. I hope someday you'll forgive me, at least enough to write me a few words. In the meantime, I will keep writing to you.

Anna wrote that you might be raising a guide dog

*puppy. Did you get it yet? Mrs. Markham has a corgi
named Foxy.*

*I am slowly learning what this country is about.
Someday I hope you will let me share it with you.*

Much love,
Dad

Lucy crushed the thin blue sheet in her fist and
stuffed it into her mouth. The letter was already on its
way through her digestive system by the time she
reached the trash bin beside the driveway. She was just
dropping the envelope into a can when a little yellow
Toyota pulled up, honking.

Anna flew out of the car to hug her. "Lucy! I made it! No more lowly freshman!"

"Yeah, now you're just lowly," Lucy said, hugging her back. But her knees were suddenly wobbly with the oddest sense of relief, like the day one winter when they'd made it to the other side of Turtle Shell Pond. Neither of them had been certain the pond was frozen all the way across. They'd taken that walk because they wanted to know what it felt like to be in "real danger." Had their world really been too safe?

Over her sister's shoulder, Lucy saw someone in the car. "Who's that?"

"Jeremy. Jeremy Hoffman. I wrote you about him, remember?"

"No, I don't." Lucy let go of Anna and stepped back. "How come Dinah didn't drive you home? Did you two have a fight or something?"

"Dinah had to stay up at school an extra day. Besides, Jeremy doesn't mind. I promised him he could stay for dinner. I bet Mom's making pesto."

Jeremy swung out of the car and came over to stand next to Anna. He had dark, shining eyes, and white, shining teeth. "Lucy! I feel like I already know you," he said. "Anna's told me so much about you."

"Oh." Lucy was thinking that tonight she and Anna wouldn't be singing "Food, Glorious Food!" like they always did when their mother cooked a special dinner. Or making obscene carrot sculptures by taking tiny bites in strategic places.

"Jeremy writes poetry, too," Anna volunteered. "I can't wait for you to get to know each other."

"Actually, I've only written a couple of poems," Jeremy said quickly. "For English assignments. Anna and I were in the same class."

"They were really, really good poems, Lu. When Jer read them in class, I practically stopped breathing! You'll see!"

Lucy blinked at her sister. Was this Anna? She sounded more like an actress in a TV commercial selling a new cereal or a vitamin. Lucy had the urge to pinch her the way she had when they were little and she'd been frustrated because she couldn't sling insults as fast as her sister.

Jeremy pulled a leaf off the mock orange bush and studied it. "Anna showed me your poem, 'Storm Queen.' It really blew me away. I'd love to read more of your stuff sometime."

"Yeah, sometime," Lucy said. She turned and raced back to the house.

"Do you want to come with us to pick up the pup tomorrow, or are you planning to sleep in?" Mrs. Rising asked Anna at dinner.

Anna turned to Lucy in amazement. "You're getting the puppy tomorrow and you didn't even tell me?"

"Oh yeah, the guide dog pup! Anna told me about that," Jeremy exclaimed. "I love dogs. Our collie, Pat, died last year. I still miss him."

Lucy looked past him and glowered at her sister. "This dog is only a temporary one," she said. "He's already a year old and he'll just be here this summer." She wondered if it was too late to tell Brenda that she'd changed her mind.

"Remember when we tried to take Zeus for a walk?" Anna asked.

In spite of herself, a slow grin began on Lucy's face. She exchanged a knowing look with her sister.

"Who's Zeus?" Jeremy was smiling like someone who didn't quite get the joke.

"A Great Dane. He belongs to our neighbors, the Schaeffers. When Lucy was six and I was eleven, we talked Mr. Schaeffer into letting us take Zeus around the block. Except, once we got out the front gate, Zeus began walking us. All we could do was hang on and follow!"

Lucy didn't correct her sister, even though Anna was rewriting history a bit. The fact was, they'd encouraged Zeus to misbehave. "Let's go wherever Zeus wants us to," Anna had whispered as soon as they were out of Mr. Schaeffer's eyesight. It was only after they'd let him lead them far away from home that Zeus had realized he was boss.

"Where did he take you?" Jeremy asked.

"At first, just in and out of neighborhood streets. But then, we got to town and he started pulling us into traffic. It was scary."

"So what did you do?"

"We tied him to a stop sign and called Mr. Schaeffer from a telephone booth. He had to come and get us."

It was still a matter of pride with Lucy that she'd done the calling. Anna had been too upset, tears crossing her face every which way like a road map.

Jeremy shook his head. "I bet you two looked really cute being pulled around by that dog. It's a good thing he didn't drag you into Turtle Shell Pond."

Lucy's breath caught in her throat, like it still did at the sound of ice cracking. What had Anna told him about the pond, she wondered? The story of their frozen crossing was one of the secrets they kept. She looked over at Anna. Her sister was blushing under Jeremy's adoring gaze.

"Jeremy, what are your plans for the summer?" Mrs. Rising asked.

Jeremy flashed his shiny grin. "Hard labor. I'm going to help build a deck onto my parents' house. My dad hired this contractor he knows and got the guy to employ me as his unskilled drudge."

Lucy watched him reach for the pasta bowl as casually as if he lived there. She grabbed it first and emptied as much as she could onto her plate. She could feel her mother's warning look.

"And my mother wants to hire Anna," Jeremy continued. "She needs someone artistic to help with stuff like refinishing furniture, picture framing, and decorating."

"Anna already has a job right next door," Lucy announced through a mouthful of spaghetti.

Anna picked up a napkin and blotted her lips. After a while it seemed to Lucy that her sister was trying to erase her mouth entirely. "Oh, Lucy, I'm tired of the party decorating business. Mrs. Schaeffer's really nice, but I want to try something different this summer."

"But you always said it was the best job in the world!" Every summer since she was twelve, Anna had helped their neighbor make flower centerpieces, balloon arches, wedding canopies, and other fancy stuff. Mrs. Schaeffer had once promised to float a balloon rainbow over the house for Lucy's sixteenth birthday.

Anna was at it with her napkin again. Above the white cloth, her blue eyes slipped sideways to meet her mother's gaze before she turned to Lucy. "I thought maybe you could work for Mrs. Schaeffer instead of me, Lu. You're old enough now. It's still the best job in the world! Besides, you're not doing anything this summer."

"I have to dog-sit!" Lucy shouted, slamming down the glass she was holding so hard the salt and pepper shakers jumped. "I've got to go to Guiding Friends meeting!" She felt like lying down on the floor. Beating her fists. Biting the table legs until she left tooth marks. She couldn't believe that Anna had waited until now to mention her change of plans. Or that her mother and sister had plotted together to force her into a job.

"I thought those meetings were just one night a week," Mrs. Rising said after a pause. "You'll have plenty of time on your hands. Besides, the Schaeffers live right next door. You can come back and check on your pup whenever you like. Maybe he can even play with Zeus."

Lucy didn't reply. She thought of Emily Dickinson, who'd written more than seventeen hundred poems. People called her a recluse. A hermit. But if she'd had to take tennis lessons or make flower centerpieces, she probably would have produced a lot less. In *The Complete Poems of Emily Dickinson*, which Mr. Frye had loaned her, Lucy had discovered a poem she was sure Emily wrote to explain why she'd shut herself away:

> *The Brain is wider than the Sky—*
> *For—put them side by side—*
> *The one the other will contain*
> *With ease—and You—beside—*

The first time she'd read it, Lucy had felt the kind of excitement that comes from finding someone who thinks and feels as you do. Emily had understood! The only place you could hold on to someone you loved was inside your head. Nowhere else was safe.

"Maybe I could ask Calvin if he wants to help Mrs. Schaeffer instead," Anna said.

Lucy pushed her chair back abruptly. It made a satisfying scraping sound, like the squeal of tires when a car turns a corner too quickly. "I'll ask him for you. I promised Calvin I'd come over for a while. Can I go now, Mom?"

Mrs. Rising gazed at Lucy without answering.

"Jeremy and I will do the dishes," Anna volunteered.

Why? Because you feel guilty for being such a big traitor? Lucy wanted to say. But she was paralyzed by her mother's look. She couldn't speak or even move, until finally Mrs. Rising broke the spell with a tiny nod. "Yes. Go on. Go."

Lucy's hand was already on the doorknob when Anna called, "Lucy? Thanks for the poem. It's really special. Maybe we can rent some James Dean movies tomorrow."

Standing on the Parkers' welcome mat, Lucy recalled one night before Anna had graduated from high school. They'd been telling secrets. She had been shocked to learn that, for years, each time Anna blew out her birthday candles, she had made the same wish: to have a friend in the house right across the street where Calvin Parker lived.

"Why in Cal's house? Why not the one next door or on the corner?" Lucy had asked, secretly thrilled to discover her sister had ever envied her for anything.

"I guess it was because I wanted exactly what you had. A best friend who was a boy. One who would understand me. It's just so . . . unusual."

Well, Anna had Jeremy now. But Lucy knew it wasn't the same. The time she spent with Cal had nothing to do with boy-girl stuff. They just always enjoyed each other's company. They both liked outdoorsy things. One spring, they'd spent all their free time inventing traps to catch a rabbit for Cal to keep as a pet. They never caught anything, but they kept on trying. At first the traps they laid were simple cardboard boxes. But after a while, they'd made them more and more elaborate, little luxury apartments with beds, snack machines, and entertainment centers. And after they'd read *My Side of the Mountain*, they'd spent months planning the wilderness camp they were going to set up someday. Lucy wanted to train a falcon to catch their food. Cal wanted to try making wild game snares.

Calvin peered out the door and blinked as if he couldn't believe Lucy was real. "I thought your sister was coming home tonight."

"She *is* home."

"Oh." Cal swung the door wider and led Lucy inside.

As they passed the living room, where her friend's mother was watching TV, Lucy called out, "Hi, Mrs. Parker."

"Lucy, we've missed you lately!"

"Me, too," Lucy mumbled. She hated how Mrs. Parker always said "we" even though there was no Mr. Parker. Cal's mother and father had never even been married. Besides, Lucy was sure Mrs. Parker didn't care one bit about her. Otherwise, she wouldn't have made Cal change schools this year.

She followed Cal to his room. He was an inch taller than Lucy, broad-shouldered, with the short, stumpy neck Lucy had noticed was common with a lot of swimmers. Swimming was one of the things Mrs. Parker had cited as a reason for sending Cal to The School for the Highly Gifted. They had a new pool and a strong team.

"So what's up with your sister?" Calvin asked, bobbing his head to the rap music blasting full force from his stereo. Last year, he'd started listening to rap because it irritated his mother. But lately, he'd told Lucy, he just listened because he liked the stuff.

"She brought home this guy. Jeremy."

Cal gave Lucy the fish eye. "So? In case you haven't noticed, I'm a guy, too."

"You don't understand." Lucy plopped down on his unmade bed. "Anna told him—Jeremy—all this personal stuff about me. Like about Guiding Friends and 'Storm Queen.' I think she might even have told him about Turtle Shell Pond."

"Probably your sister doesn't think it's such a big deal anymore. It happened years ago, Lucy. You didn't even drown." Cal let a high-pitched giggle escape.

Lucy had never admitted to Anna that she was wrong about Cal. He didn't exactly understand her. It was more like he *accepted* her. To Calvin, what happened at Turtle Shell Pond was simple. Lucy and Anna had risked their safety—maybe even their lives—as a kind of ultimate challenge. But to Lucy, it was more complicated. Mysterious. She could still remember the white puffs their breath had made as she and Anna inched their way across the ice. Those puffs drifted toward each other and became one before they disappeared. Cal was right. She hadn't died. But when she'd reached the far side of the pond, Lucy felt she'd been changed forever, even though she couldn't exactly say how.

Cal sat down on the floor and leaned his back

against the bed. "Look, everyone's sensitive about their childhood. Remember the time in second grade when I stole a bottle of hair straightener from Curl Up and Dye? My hair was so blonde and curly, the kids called me Goldilocks. I was hanging up my jacket at the back of the classroom and Miss Robertson saw the bottle sticking out of my pocket. I thought I was going to jail for sure. Now my mother tells the story to her customers like it's some funny little anecdote. It makes me furious."

Lucy closed her eyes and recalled the day. Two seven-year-olds trudging home through fall leaves. Cal weighted down by the note in his backpack.

Dear Mrs. Parker:
Calvin brought a bottle of hair relaxer to school today. At first he told me you'd accidentally put it in his pocket. Later on, he admitted he'd taken it from your salon because he hates his curls. I think they're adorable! In this case, I believe the punishment is best left to the parent and not the teacher.

Sincerely,
Elsa Jean Robertson, Teacher, Class 2A

All the way home, Cal had bawled about what his mother was going to do to him. Still, on the next-to-last block, he'd uncapped the bottle and had Lucy pour it over his head. He had to try it, he'd said, since he was already in trouble anyway. Lucy loved that part best.

Maybe Cal was right. Maybe Turtle Shell Pond was just one of those childhood experiences that seemed like a bigger deal than it really was. Suddenly, Lucy felt like a sniveling baby, so she didn't say what else she'd been thinking. That it wasn't right for her sister to be acting like things were normal. That Anna's life was supposed to have stopped, too.

"You want to do something tomorrow?" Cal asked.

Lucy was grateful for a change of subject. "I almost forgot! I'm picking up a dog tomorrow from Guiding Friends."

"Great! We can take it to town and walk it in and out of the stores, just to annoy the salespeople."

Lucy laughed. "You can't do that. This booklet I've got from Guiding Friends says you've got to ask permission first. Storekeepers don't have to let the trainee dogs in if they don't want to." She saw Cal's tongue peek out from the corner of his mouth like it always did when he was up to something.

"I'll just bring a notepad along and tell them Guiding Friends asked us to make a list of businesses to support and businesses to avoid for the local paper."

"You're too much!" Lucy shook her head. "We're picking up the dog at ten tomorrow. I'll call you when we get back." As she got up, she remembered something else. "Oh. Anna wants me to ask if you want a summer job helping Mrs. Schaeffer. She's going to work for Jeremy's mother, instead." She made the word *Jeremy* sound distasteful.

"Well, do I?" Cal asked.

Lucy felt a rush of gratitude so forceful she had to look away. She and Calvin used to beg Anna to let them help her at Mrs. Schaeffer's. *For free.*

"Actually, I was thinking Mrs. Schaeffer might let us share the job." Lucy pretended not to notice the smile that was breaking out on Cal's face. "Anna's always loved working there, and we'd have a lot of spending money by the end of the summer."

"Yes!" Cal gave Lucy an enthusiastic high five.

Lucy was surprised to find she was feeling quite pleased, too.

From the Parkers' doorstep, Lucy checked her driveway. Jeremy's car was gone. Her shoulders relaxed into their usual slouch as she crossed the street. Ahead, the fireflies stirred and rose, blinking like the lights of a fairy city. She reached out and captured one in her fist, carrying it into the kitchen where her mother kept clean mayonnaise jars.

"Remember when we used to catch these?" she asked, hesitating in the doorway to her sister's room.

Anna was lying on her bed with a book in her hand, staring out the window. When she turned and glimpsed the peace offering, her mouth opened in delight. "A firefly! Come in and shut off the light." She scooted over so Lucy could stretch out next to her.

Silently, they watched the jar until the beetle lit up. "Are you still mad at me?" Anna asked.

"No. Yes. I don't know." Lucy smiled to herself, knowing each answer was the truth. She picked up her sister's old teddy and stroked its shabby fur. "You talked to Mom about me behind my back."

"No, I didn't. Mom talked to me." When Lucy rolled her eyes, Anna exclaimed, "There's a difference! Mom's worried you're going to spend the summer moping around. She's the one who thought of asking you to work for Mrs. Schaeffer. All I did was mention that Jeremy's mother wanted to hire me."

"You talked to Jeremy about me, too. You told him about Guiding Friends. You even let him read my poem."

"Lucy! I was proud of you! I wanted to share it with someone I cared about. Besides, that poem was published. Anyone can read it now."

Her sister's answers made Lucy want to put her fingers in her ears. She wondered why it was that the more reasonable Anna became, the more she wanted to act like a little kid. "You wrote to Dad about me!" she burst out. "Just like a stinking spy!" Really, she didn't even want to be mad at Anna, but she couldn't seem to stop herself.

"I had to do it! Dad asks about you in every letter, Lucy. I couldn't ignore him, and you won't write to him yourself."

"*You had to,*" Lucy echoed. "You just can't help being Anna the Responsible. And I'll always be Lucy the Emotional. Too sensitive. Too difficult." She couldn't help it that so many things made her eyes well up. The tiny crocuses that poked up their heads like baby birds around Turtle Shell Pond every spring. A homeless man she'd seen in the city wearing only one shoe.

Nor could she keep her prickly feelings at bay. When Anna got to wear the blueberry mohair sweater their father left behind, just because it matched her eyes, Lucy had raged inside. Now it seemed there were other ways Anna was like him besides blueberry eyes.

"Come on, Lucy, that's not it! I just gave him a few little details. I didn't think you'd mind so much." Anna lifted herself up on one elbow abruptly. "Anyway, how do you know that I wrote to Dad about you?"

"I got a letter from him today."

Lucy watched her sister's face brighten. She knew exactly how Anna felt. Dad had held the pen that touched the paper. He'd licked the stamp. It might be stained with coffee he'd been drinking while he wrote.

Anna snapped on her bedside light. "Can I read it?"

Lucy could feel bits of paper fluttering around her stomach like a tiny snowstorm. "I don't have it any-more."

"You threw it away? Outside? I'll go get it."

"I didn't trash it. I ate it."

Forever after, Lucy knew, this moment would be frozen in time. The white curtains would be bowed in the summer breeze. The firefly would be permanently aglow. And Anna would be staring at her with eyes that were perfect blue marbles.

As if she finally understood, Anna whispered, "You mean you swallowed it?"

"Yes."

"Did you ever do it before? With other letters?"

"Yes."

"How many all together?"

"Six."

"Oh, my God, Lucy!"

Anna rocked back and forth, cradling her head in her hands. Seeing her that way made Lucy wince, yet at the same time, she felt a touch of pride. Now who was the emotional one? Of course Lucy knew eating mail was not exactly normal, but it seemed like Anna was overreacting. Had her sister already forgotten the day they'd skipped lunch and gone to the park, eating clover, dandelions, and a few ants, just to see if they could survive in the wild?

"Why?" Anna whispered.

"Because I couldn't throw them away. I mean, writing comes from inside a person. Like blood, or tears. Even though I hate Dad, I couldn't just dispose of his words in a trash can."

Through whitened lips, Anna asked, "Why couldn't you keep them in a drawer?"

"I didn't want to have to see them again." It was not the whole truth, but it seemed to Lucy that her sister wasn't ready to hear the rest.

Lucy was amazed at how geometrical Hobart appeared. He had a square head, a rectangular body, and a ruler-straight tail that rose and fell like a toll gate. He was as black and shiny as a crow's feather.

"Why is he panting?" she asked Brenda. "Is he thirsty?"

Brenda leaned over her desk to pat the dog's head. "Nervous, more likely. And he probably misses his foster family—imagine how you'd feel if your mom and dad just disappeared."

Lucy reached out and began stroking Hobart's sleek back. When the dog turned and met her eyes, she whispered, "It's okay, boy."

"What we look for in a dog is a balance between self-confidence and obedience," Brenda explained. "A guide dog must be willing to do what is asked, but it must also be able to make decisions on its own. These dogs are under quite a lot of pressure. They take buses and trains during rush hour. They're subjected to screeching brakes, honking horns, blaring sirens, and the roar of the subway. They get stepped on by commuters, bumped by automatic doors. Steam from manhole covers blows in their faces, not to mention rain, sleet, and snow. They have to be able to handle it all without panicking."

"Getting stuck in rush hour makes me a nervous wreck," Lucy's mother told Brenda. "How does a dog learn to stand it?"

"The dogs we use are bred for their natural courage and steadiness. It's a raiser's job to help those qualities blossom. Later, if the dog shows promise, we'll take it into the professional training program."

The wall behind Brenda's desk was covered with photographs of guide dogs wearing official-looking leather harnesses. Each dog was posed against a sky blue background like the ones used in school portraits, and their names were etched into little brass plates that were mounted on the frames. Lucy tried to concentrate on reading those names: Scout, Radar, Hero, Champ, Buddy, Blazer. Still, she couldn't stop herself from asking, "What happens to the dogs that don't seem 'promising'?"

"Those that don't pass their final evaluations are released."

Anna gasped. "You mean the poor things flunk out?"

Brenda's smile was amused. "Not exactly. Some terrific dogs are just not tempermentally suited for this kind of work. They may be selected for other careers. Working for law enforcement agencies. In therapy programs. Some just become house pets."

Lucy hesitated. "Does Hobart seem . . . suited to be a guide dog?"

Brenda raised her eyebrows and her shoulders in one motion. She made Lucy think of a marionette being pulled by the strings. "Even though we're continually evaluating the dogs from the time they're born, it's too early to tell. Some dogs take a little longer to develop—just like some people."

"Is Hobart one of those?" Anna asked.

Brenda did her marionette shrug again. "At his last few classes, the trainer thought he was still a bit soft. It's nothing serious."

"Soft?" Lucy repeated.

"Unsure of himself." Brenda seemed hesitant to say more.

"Wimpy," Anna added.

Brenda held out a thick yellow envelope. "You'll learn more when you bring Hobart to class each week. It meets on Wednesdays. In the meantime, this packet of information will help explain the process." She gave Hobart a final pat on the head. "Good luck."

Hobart didn't seem interested in the house tour Lucy was giving him. In the kitchen, she showed him the stainless steel bowls for his food and water and offered him a cool drink. He put his tongue in the water and lapped a bit. Then he looked up as if to ask, "Was that enough?"

"Don't be so wishy-washy," Lucy told him. "You've got to decide for yourself." If Hobart was going to act uncertain about how much water to drink, she wondered, how could he ever decide if it was safe to cross the street? She thought of Zeus, who hadn't seemed at all indecisive when he'd pulled Anna and her into the road. Was it better to be indecisive or impulsive? In her family, her father had been the impulsive one. Her mother had called him irresponsible. Once he'd come home in a teeny red sports car. "Who wants the first ride?" he'd shouted, pulling into the driveway.

Lucy could still feel the pinch of her mother's fingers on her shoulder, holding her back. "I thought we'd agreed on a *family* car, Dan. A wagon or a van."

"This one's on sale. Come on, it's just for a test drive." Lucy's father had grinned his special grin, the one Mrs. Rising said could melt ice cream at the North Pole. Lucy had watched her mother skip down the three steps to the front walk and climb in beside her dad. She hadn't even looked back. Lucy had stood on tiptoe at the curb long after they were out of sight, wondering if they'd ever return.

"Come on, Hobart, I'll show you my room." She led the dog upstairs, but when she walked into her room, he was no longer behind her. "Hobart?" She spun around. He was standing just outside the doorway, staring up at her.

"It's okay to come in. This is your room now, too," she told him. When he still didn't move, she tried speaking in a firmer voice. "Hobart, come here!"

Hobart padded in to stand at Lucy's side, but he kept his head down as if he were nervous or ashamed. Lucy crouched down and spoke to him in a gentle, crooning voice. "Good dog. I just want you to see where you'll be staying tonight. Look, you can sleep on this rug." To give him the right idea, she stretched out on it herself. Hobart stood over her, eyes locked on her face. His doggy breath reminded her a bit of the garlicky smoked meats her father used to buy in the deli.

She tried to understand what was going on inside his big, boxy head. It was still morning—maybe he just wasn't tired enough to lie down. Or perhaps he'd never even been allowed on a rug before. She knew Guiding Friends dogs weren't supposed to get up on the beds or other furniture, although Brenda hadn't said anything about floor coverings.

Or maybe Hobart was just afraid Lucy would disappear if he closed his eyes for a second?

She rubbed him behind the ear and whispered the command. "Down."

Instantly, Hobart collapsed on the rug beside her. Lucy let out a little gasp. She'd uttered only a single word. She'd said it softly. And yet, the dog had obeyed her as quickly as if she'd brandished a whip. Now the whip wrapped itself around her own chest. What if she told him to do the wrong thing? To lie down, when he really needed to scratch? To be quiet, when he knew a burglar was lurking behind the hedges? To quit chasing the neighbor's cat, when it had just clawed his nose?

She stared at the wall across the room where a huge, dog-shaped shadow rose. It loomed above Lucy like a giant in a fairy tale. She couldn't help wondering if this was how parents felt about their children. Over-whelmed. Scared.

Hobart snuggled closer into her side. His breathing had become steady and peaceful. Lucy decided to remain on the floor for a little while so he wouldn't have to get up and follow her around. She reached over to her bed and picked up the fat information packet she'd gotten from Brenda. Just the idea of reading it was exhausting.

"Lucy, the phone! Didn't you hear?" Anna was standing in the doorway.

"I was reading this booklet. I guess I fell asleep." Lucy dragged herself up and lifted the receiver. "Hello?"

"Hi!" It was Calvin. "Did you get it?"

"Him. His name is Hobart."

"What's he like?"

Lucy looked down at Hobart, who was resting his chin on her toes. "He's okay."

"Let's go show him around town."

"All right. I'll meet you outside in two minutes." Lucy hung up and gave Hobart a pat. "Come on, let's get you ready."

Downstairs, she slipped on the choke collar Hobart needed to wear when he went out. Lucy hated the name of the thing, but the Guiding Friends pamphlet had explained that a choke would teach the dog to be a good walker. Whenever Hobart pulled too hard, the choke would tighten around his neck, reminding him to slow down.

There were other rules about taking Hobart out, too. He was supposed to walk on the left at all times. He had to learn to ignore temptations, such as other dogs and cats, even if they crossed in front of his nose. And then there was the "get busy!" command. According to the pamphlet, guide dogs were taught to "eliminate on command" because blind people couldn't actually see whether or not their dog had done its business. Lucy thought if anyone overheard her telling Hobart to get busy, she would die of embarrassment.

Cal was waiting on the sidewalk. He crouched down as Lucy and Hobart approached. "How do you do, Hobart?" When the dog placed a big paw on his palm, Cal giggled.

"Didn't you start summer swim practice at the Town Park this morning?" Lucy asked.

"Uh-huh. It was cool. Most of the kids were on the Town Rec team last summer, so I already knew them. And the coach isn't as strict as the one at school, which is fine with me. We fooled around a lot and he didn't even complain."

Calvin wanted everyone to think he wasn't serious about swimming. Or anything else, for that matter. But Lucy knew it was just an act. Last year, before he'd changed schools, she'd come to one of his meets. The final seconds before he dove off the side had given him away. His face had taken on a determined look, and his body had become taut and still. Lucy had found herself holding her own breath until he reached the other side, several strokes before anyone else.

Later that night she'd written a poem.

CAL'S DREAM

While the moon hung like a fisherman's hook,
he dove down deep as midnight sleep,
wound through caves of creamy coral,
glided over eely grass,
hitched a ride on the turtle's back,
laughed a trail of shimmering bubbles,
all the way to his kingdom keep.

The guards at the gate had nutcracker claws,
but they let him pass without a pinch
He entered the castle of pearly shells,
wished on the starfish that winked through the
    window,
slept in a hammock of woven reed,
woke to the sound of the lonely gull,
caught a ride home on the long tide's pull.

Lucy had never shown the poem to Cal, because he couldn't stand anyone thinking he was special. She thought it might be because it made him feel too much pressure. After *Freestyle* came out with her poem in it, she couldn't write anything for days.

They strolled past a hedge of sweet blooming lilac.

Hobart kept poking his nose into the bushes as if he'd never smelled anything so wonderful. Lucy picked a blossom and stuck it through one of the links of his choke collar. So far, Hobart hadn't pulled at all. She wondered if he was always so well behaved or if he was afraid she'd leave him if he wasn't good. She wished he'd act up just a little. She wanted him to know it would be okay with her.

"Did you tell Anna we'll take the job?" Cal asked.

"Yes, at breakfast. She said she'd talk to Mrs. Schaeffer about us when she gets back this afternoon"—Lucy wrinkled her nose in disgust—"from Jeremy's."

Cal ignored her scornful tone. "Great. I really need the money." He nodded toward Frozen Dreams on the other side of the street. "You want to stop for ice cream?"

"If you'd quit spending all your money on food, maybe you wouldn't need a job." Lucy stopped in her tracks. In front of the store was a figure she knew, even though she'd never seen him in khaki shorts and a T-shirt before. "Look! It's my English teacher, Mr. Frye."

"Frye? As in French fry?" When he noticed Lucy's disgusted look, Cal added, "I can't help it. I'm starving!"

"He's the one who got my poem published in *Freestyle*," Lucy whispered.

"Aren't you going to say hello?"

Lucy hesitated. She didn't want to have to tell Mr.

Frye about her plans for the summer. He had a way of listening that sometimes made you say more than you'd meant to. But Hobart surprised her with a gentle but definite pull in the teacher's direction.

"Look, he sees a fellow Labradorian," Cal pointed out.

Lucy glanced again at Mr. Frye. He was grasping the leash of a bouncy black Lab, which was wagging its tail excitedly. "Okay, Hobart, forward," she said.

"Hello, Lucy!" Mr. Frye called as they approached. "I guess even a Storm Queen can enjoy a beautiful day once in a while. I promised Chaucer a walk and some ice cream." He nodded toward his dog.

"This is Hobart," Lucy said. When Cal poked her in the ribs, she added, "And this is my friend Calvin."

"Nice to meet you, Calvin. And you too, Hobart." Mr. Frye gave the dog a pat. "Do you like vanilla ice cream? It's Chaucer's favorite."

"I don't think he's ever tried it," Lucy said. "He's not supposed to have any people food. He's in training to be a guide dog for the blind. I'm helping him get ready for the program."

"He seems pretty well trained already," Mr. Frye said.

Lucy felt a twinge of embarrassment. While Chaucer strained at his leash, wiggling and wagging, Hobart had retreated behind her and was pressing his head into the backs of her knees. "He needs his self-confidence built up," she explained.

"I see." Mr. Frye studied Hobart thoughtfully. Then he asked, "Have you been writing, Lucy?"

"I, uh, I'm planning to—when I have time." Lucy stumbled over the words. He couldn't mean her father's unanswered letters, could he?

"Good. I'm taking over as teacher-advisor to *Freestyle* next fall. I hope you'll think about joining the editorial staff. In the meantime, if you want to send me anything you write over the summer, I'll be happy to read it. That way I'll get a head start on things." He turned to Calvin. "Are you a poet, too?"

Cal gave a little shrug. "Sort of."

Lucy couldn't believe her ears. As far as she knew, Cal had never written a poem in his life.

"You're welcome to submit your work, too. We're always looking for new voices," Mr. Frye told him.

"Thanks, but I don't go to your school." Cal gazed at his feet. "I'm a student at SHG."

"The School for the Highly Gifted?" Mr. Frye rolled his bottom lip out as if he were impressed. "Well, I'm sure they have a terrific literary magazine."

"Yeah."

Mr. Frye reached into his wallet and extracted a little white card, which he handed to Lucy. "Here's my address in case you want to send me anything."

"Okay." Lucy took the card without looking at it and stuffed it into the pocket of her shorts.

"Well, it was nice to see you—and you too, boy." Mr. Frye crouched down in front of Hobart. The dog plopped a big paw on his knee. "Very good! You could teach Chaucer some manners." The teacher laughed. "Come on, Chaucer, it's time to go home."

Lucy watched Hobart's big, soft eyes follow Chaucer down the street. Then she turned to Cal. "Since when do you write poetry?"

"All the time. Up here." Cal tapped his head.

Lucy squinted at him skeptically. Cal had always been very smart, but his mother complained he was lazy. It was another one of her reasons for sending him to SHG this year. Lucy didn't think Cal was lazy, though. Just particular. If Cal was interested in something, he could work longer and harder than anyone. She was certain he could write reams of poetry if he wanted to.

"Come on. Let's get some ice cream," Lucy said, turning toward Frozen Dreams. "I feel like chocolate ripple, and Hobie will have a cup of vanilla."

"You mean we're taking Hobart inside?" Cal asked.

"Mm-hmm."

"I thought we had to ask permission first. Anyway, didn't you say he isn't supposed to have people food?"

Lucy shrugged. "He needs to feel loved, even if it means breaking a few rules."

Cal grinned. "Hey, want to hear a poem about ice cream?" Before Lucy even answered, he pushed open the door to the store chanting, "I scream, you scream, we all scream, for ice cream!"

7

Cal had to stop at Curl Up and Dye, his mother's salon. Mrs. Parker liked to tell people that Cal, who'd suggested the name after hearing it in a movie, had inherited her sense of humor. Lucy continued on home with Hobart. She hoped Anna was back. She wanted to tell her about meeting Mr. Frye and his invitation to join the *Freestyle* staff. Anna would probably say something like, "An editor? I bet you think you're hot stuff. I bet you think I'm going to make your bed and clean your room and lend you my red bikini. Well, in this house you're still one of the little people and don't forget it!" Then she'd smack Lucy on the rear end to let her know she wasn't serious.

But the yellow Toyota was parked in the driveway again. Lucy walked Hobart over and let him sniff. "Get busy!" she commanded. The dog lifted his leg obligingly and squirted a long yellow stream down Jeremy's right front tire. "Good dog!" Lucy praised him.

She slipped into the house, hoping to escape upstairs without being detected. From the hallway she could see into the living room. Anna and Jeremy sat close together on the couch facing the fireplace, a photo album spread across their laps. Lucy could tell that they hadn't heard her come in. "This is my father and me at the circus," Anna said in a hoarse voice. "A clown took the picture. Just the two of us went because Lucy was afraid of clowns. Mom stayed home with her."

Lucy watched Jeremy pull Anna closer and kiss her hair, her eyes, and her mouth. She felt sick to her stomach, but she couldn't stop looking, either. She had the strangest sense that she'd dematerialized into thin air.

Hobart whined softly. Anna dabbed at her eyes and turned around. "Lucy, hi! I didn't hear you come in."

"Hi, Lucy. Hey, what a great dog!" Jeremy came over and scratched Hobart behind the ears. To Lucy's disgust, Hobart rolled over onto his back.

"He likes you, Jer!" Anna exclaimed.

Lucy narrowed her eyes at her sister. It seemed like Anna's brain had dematerialized permanently. "He likes everybody," Lucy told her. "On the way home, he rolled over in front of Hannibal Lechter."

Jeremy laughed. "We were just talking about you, Lucy."

Gee, it looked more like lip reading, a voice in her head whispered. She cleared her throat. "Really?"

"The County Fair's next weekend. We thought maybe you'd go with us."

Still grasping the leash, Lucy pulled Hobart out of Jeremy's reach. "Thanks, but I don't really like fairs." She didn't mention that last year their whole family had gone, and she noticed Anna didn't either. It hadn't exactly been a Brady Bunch outing. In the car, Lucy had sat up front with their father. Anna had sat in the back with their mother. It was the same at the fairgrounds. Lucy and Mr. Rising went to the rodeo events. Anna and Mrs. Rising went to the flower and vegetable exhibits. On the way home, Lucy had complained of a headache. Her mother blamed it on all the sweet stuff her father had let her eat.

"Why don't you loosen up, Lainie? All I did was buy my daughter an ice cream and a soda at the fair. You're acting like I poisoned her." Her father's voice had been strong and angry, but before he'd answered, Lucy had seen a wounded look pass over his face. She'd wanted to throw her arms around his neck and tell him she felt fine now.

"All that sugar *is* like poison, but you don't care, do you, Daniel? You just want to be the good guy!"

"I guess I can't ever do anything right, can I?"

"Stop it! Stop it! Stop yelling at each other!" Lucy had screamed. *"Being in this family is what gives me a headache!"*

"Come on, Lucy! I read in the paper there's a forty-foot water slide this year. It'll be fun," Anna urged.

"I can't go. I have to be here to walk Hobie."

"Ask Mom. Or Calvin. We really want to spend the day with you. Please!"

Lucy wasn't fooled. This trip to the fair was a plot Anna had concocted, probably so Jeremy could win her over. Lucy also knew her sister would never give up—until she gave in.

She crossed her fingers behind her back. "Okay, okay, I'll go."

"Great! We can leave at . . ."

Lucy didn't hear the rest because she was already hurrying upstairs. She could hardly breathe as she flipped the switch and waited for The Great Eye to blink awake. Then she began typing.

REJECTION NOTICE
Dear Miss Rising,
We are sorry to inform you
that you are no longer needed
around here. You see,
so many people
have applied for your job
and while no one is quite like you
there are quite a few who are,
shall we say,
easier
or perhaps, not so demanding.
More appreciative, cooperative, thoughtful
helpful, generous, kinder, and mature,
not to mention likeable.
Everyone deserves a chance—
You've had yours.
We are quite certain
you will have no trouble
finding another family.

As soon as Lucy opened her eyes each morning, she remembered. Not that words formed in her head; it was more of a feeling. Like being covered by a heavy old quilt—one with a mind of its own. When Lucy dragged herself out of bed, it refused to stay back with the crumpled sheets and damp pillows. Instead, it flung itself around her shoulders like a cape.

But this morning—Monday—the first thing Lucy felt was air. A warm, misty cloud like the bathroom after she showered. Only this cloud smelled funny—like dog breath! She opened her eyes and found herself facing a quivering snout. A tongue like a slippery eel emerged and licked her on the eyebrow, the nose, and the cheek.

"Hobart, stop!" Lucy slid under the covers. The dog lifted the blanket with his nose and continued licking.

"Hobie . . . enough!" Lucy squealed. Instead, Hobart seemed encouraged by her laughter. He licked her ear and then started on her neck, as if he were determined to give her a thorough scouring. She squirmed until she fell out of bed.

"Lucy, everything okay?" Mrs. Rising poked her head

in the door. She smiled down at her daughter, sprawled on the floor. Hobart began pulling at Lucy's pajama sleeve.

"I'm great, Mom. But I think Hobie has to go."

"Looks that way," Mrs. Rising agreed. "I've got to run. Today's the first day of camp. I can't wait to meet the kids."

Lucy turned her attention to her mother. Her hair was pulled up in a ponytail. She wore a red T-shirt that said Camp Rise 'N' Shine and showed a picture of a little kid in a wheelchair on his way up a mountain. She also had on a pair of snug black shorts, which made her look young and attractive. Lucy wished her father could see her mother like this.

"It's my first day, too," she said, sitting up. "Mrs. Schaeffer wants Cal and me to help make decorations for a baby shower. Cal's afraid she's going to ask us to knit booties."

"He'd probably be great at it. Cal's a real Renaissance man. Remember that journal he made for your birthday one year? He covered it in red velvet himself! Someday he'll probably make a great dad. The kind of guy who can run a business and bake the chocolate chips." Mrs. Rising looked at her watch. "Gotta run! Don't forget you and Hobie have class tonight. Say hi to Mrs. Schaeffer!"

"I will." As Lucy pulled on her cutoffs, she tried to remember if her father had ever made chocolate chip cookies. She was pretty sure he hadn't. Cal's mother ran Curl Up and Dye and baked great applesauce muffins. Did that make Mrs. Parker a Renaissance woman? What did it have to do with being a good parent, anyway?

"I feel like a flower abuser," Cal said. "Look at all these little guys. First they're dyed baby blue, as if their natural color isn't good enough. Then we cut off their stems and stick them with wires. I bet we get busted by the ASPCF or something."

"The American Society for the Prevention of Cruelty to Flowers?" Lucy wrapped a piece of green floral tape around the wire stem of a carnation. "Next I suppose you'll start feeling sorry for weeds."

"As a matter of fact, I do sympathize with them. Weeds are only flowers that have been rejected by society." Cal sniffed. "Come on, let's start attaching these to the carriage."

"In a minute." Lucy pulled her hair back and wound it with a piece of floral wire the way she'd seen Anna do dozens of times. This morning, standing on the Schaeffers' doorstep, she'd felt like Anna's kid sister. Too young and too dumb to be much help. She'd figured Mrs. Schaeffer had hired her just to do her mom a favor. But their neighbor had been so businesslike, showing Lucy and Cal the white wicker baby carriage that was to be covered in blue carnations. Then, after she'd demonstrated how to prepare the blossoms, she'd announced she was going out.

Lucy had just stared, wide-eyed.

"I have to pick up a helium tank and balloons. Don't worry, you'll do fine without me," Mrs. Schaeffer had said reassuringly. She picked up her purse and left, before Lucy could disagree.

Cal grabbed the handle of the carriage and rocked it a bit. "You think they're actually going to put a baby in this thing? It seems pretty rickety."

"No, they're just going to fill it with presents for the baby shower." Lucy poked the wire stem of a carnation through the carriage's hood. "The baby will probably get one of those modern strollers that its parents can jog with."

Cal began fixing flowers to the other side of the hood. "When I'm a father, I'm going to carry my kid in a backpack. That way I'll be close enough to explain everything he sees."

"Or she. You know, this morning my mother said you're going to make a great father."

"She did?"

"Uh-huh." Lucy couldn't help noticing how wide Cal's grin was, like he'd just won a year's supply of junk food. "She called you a Renaissance man, whatever that means."

"A Renaissance man is a guy who's into arty stuff in addition to his regular business. Like Thomas Jefferson wasn't just the author of the Constitution. He was also an architect, a musician, and a terrific gardener. Ow! I stuck myself." Cal popped an injured forefinger into his mouth. When he pulled it out again, he added, "I guess your mom thinks child rearing is like an art."

Lucy didn't answer. She held a carnation between her teeth while she fixed another to the carriage.

Cal bent down and peeked under their workbench. "Poor Hobart, you're not having much fun, are you? Zeus isn't a very good playmate. All he does is sleep."

"Mrs. Schaeffer says it's because Zeus is pretty old —fifteen—for a dog. Anyway, Hobart's going to obedience class tonight. He can make friends there."

"What he needs is disobedience class. He's hardly moved from under the table. Aren't puppies supposed to be more active?"

"He's a year old. He's not a puppy," Lucy said. She pulled another wire through the wicker. "Besides, I think maybe he's trying to figure out what's happened to him. His whole life just changed."

"What is he, a dog—or a philosopher? I don't know if canines are really that smart, Lu." But when Cal looked into Lucy's defiant face, he added, "Okay, maybe you're right."

The door to the workshop swung open and Mrs. Schaeffer poked her head in. "Could you two come out and help me unload the . . ." She stopped in midsentence and eyed the carriage. "What a fabulous job! The spacing is perfect, and the flowers don't even have that overhandled look. You two are off to a great start."

Her delight swept Lucy up like a petal on a breeze. She tucked a carnation behind her ear. Then she wiped her hands on her shorts and followed Mrs. Schaeffer out to the car.

By twelve-thirty, Mrs. Schaeffer had taken off with the flowered carriage in the back of her van. Lucy still had the entire afternoon to write—no one to bug her about getting fresh air or exercise or socializing. She sat down in her desk chair and flipped the red switch on. Like a blue-eyed genie, the screen blinked open.

Hi, Eye. Do you think if I asked Dad to make me some chocolate chip cookies, he would? she typed.

Hmhmhmhmhmhmhmhmhmhmhmhmhmhmhmhmhmh mhmhmhmhmhmhm.

Yeah, that's what you always say.

If her mother knew she was talking to her computer, Lucy was sure she would have had a fit. Mrs. Rising was always worrying about how much time she spent at the keyboard. It was because of what Mrs. Freedy, the school psychologist, had said. That Lucy's poetry was a "healthy way to dispel her feelings—as long as her writing didn't take the place of 'normal adolescent activities.'"

"Mom, she's making it sound as if poetry writing is abnormal!" Lucy had raged, when her mother had related the discussion. "She's nothing but a . . . a Philistine!" (This was a word Lucy had heard Cal use to describe his mother after she'd made him shut off one of his rap tapes. "Only a Philistine would deprive her son of a little culture, Ma!") But for a week after Mrs. Freedy's pronouncement, Lucy's mother had organized a different activity every night. Tie-dyeing T-shirts. Making terrariums out of empty Coke bottles. Watching old movie musicals like *Flower Drum Song* (dumb) and *My Fair Lady* (okay). Listening to a tape that taught beginning Japanese. Even taking tap-dancing lessons on videocassette! Finally, Lucy had had to lock herself in her room and refuse to come out until her mother agreed to leave her to her writing.

Through the window over her desk, she could see the postman stuffing the mailbox at the bottom of the driveway. The sight made her groan. It was no use. She jumped up from her chair and ran downstairs. It didn't take long for her to find the feathery blue envelope with the ostrich on the stamp.

Dear Lucy:

You are probably surprised to hear from me again so soon, but I wanted you to know that I will be on vacation for the next two weeks, so you won't be able to reach me. Mrs. Markham—Sarah—and I are going on a camping trip into the outback. Don't worry! We've hired a guide to see that we don't get lost. His name is Lefty—I know you'll think that's funny. I've got my camera and lots of film so I can take pictures to send you. We're supposed to be seeing all kinds of wildlife, including crocodiles. In fact, we are leaving Foxy home because crocodiles

*especially like to eat small dogs. I'll be keeping a journal,
which I'll share with you, too, although now that you're a
published writer, I'm worried that I won't be able to
measure up to your standards.*

*I have spent a whole week shopping to get ready. New
hiking boots, a bush shirt made of canvas, long socks to
keep the scorpions off, shorts with half a dozen pockets,
and a big leather hat that's so heavy, it makes my neck sit
crooked. I haven't been so excited in years!*

*Even while I'm gone, I'll be thinking of you, trying to
imagine what your reaction would be to each new sight.*

> *Much love,*
> *Dad*

Once, on a class trip to the museum, Lucy had passed
a case of shrunken heads. The mouths on their tiny,
shriveled faces were contorted in expressions of horror
and pain. While her classmates squealed or cracked
jokes, Lucy had unfocused her eyes the way she'd
learned to do when she didn't really want to see something. Now she wondered where those heads had come
from. Africa? Or was it Australia? She wished she'd
paid attention.

Lucy crushed the letter in her fist until it was no
bigger than a shrunken head. But halfway to her lips
she changed her mind. Instead, she smoothed out the
paper and ripped it down the middle. She stuffed one

half in her pocket. Then she swallowed the other half
and ran upstairs.

HELLO, FEDERAL

I just wanted to ask
Before E-mail, the fax, the phone
and overnight delivery anywhere on the planet
In the days of the singing telegram
carrier pigeon
telegraph
Pony Express
African drumbeat
Indian smoke signal
and caveman pictures
was there still
Return to Sender?
It seems to me only fair
that words can be returned
unseen, unsung, unsmoked
unopened, because—
once you get the message
it's hard to keep your heart
from answering back

"Are you sure you don't mind if I don't come in?" Lucy's mother asked. "I'm just so exhausted. If I'd remembered what five-year-olds were like this morning, I wouldn't have told Anna that she could stay for dinner at Jeremy's. I'd have asked her to come home so she could go to Hobart's class with you."

Lucy shrugged. "It doesn't matter. See you at eight." She slipped out of the car and led Hobie away before her mother could reconsider. The church where the class was held was the picture-postcard kind. Even though it was summer, Lucy could imagine its pointed roof blanketed in snow, sunlight twinkling from the steeple like a morning star. On another day, she might have stopped to write a poem about it.

She found the gate in the white picket fence and swung it open. Hobie picked up his pace. He seemed to know where to go, so Lucy let him lead her to the side entrance and down the basement stairs.

"Come on in, Lucy!" Brenda said. "We're just about to begin." The "we" were about ten other dog-and-raiser pairs. They were all standing in a line facing Brenda. As Lucy walked by, each dog strained at its leash, trying to land a friendly lick on Hobie.

It was a bit like a family reunion, Lucy thought. A

gathering of relatives at Thanksgiving dinner, everyone filled with happy anticipation.

"This is Lucy Rising, Hobart's new raiser," Brenda told the group. She turned to Lucy. "Hobart already knows everyone here, and so will you by the end of the evening. Just watch what the others do and follow along. We'll begin with the down-and-stay."

The participants coaxed, commanded, and in some cases threatened their dogs into obeying. Hobart just plopped right down the instant he heard the woman next to Lucy give her dog the down command. Lucy hadn't even spoken to him yet! Hobart made her think of Mr. Waggy, the remote-control beagle she'd received for her fourth birthday. When you pressed his remote button once, he walked forward. Twice, he sat. Three times and he dropped to the floor—just like Hobart. Lucy crossed the room to where the other raisers were grouped, scowling to herself. Hobart didn't need any more classes. *He* was training *her*.

After a few seconds, one of the dogs, a black Lab like Hobart, ran over to a gray-haired woman in sneakers and a T-shirt that said "Sexy Senior Citizen."

"No, no, Midnight! Bad boy! You're supposed to stay," the woman exclaimed.

"Bring him back to the line and try again, Grace," Brenda said.

Before Grace could get control of Midnight, a golden retriever came bounding across the floor.

"Comanche, no! Stay!" scolded the boy next to Lucy.

He was lanky, brown-skinned, and the only person in the class besides Lucy who wasn't an adult. He turned to her and shook his head. "Goldens!"

Lucy looked back at Hobart. He was lying flat with his head between his paws watching the action. The rest of the dogs were either standing and barking or galloping around the room. If Hobart had been a kid, Lucy thought, his classmates would have called him a goody-goody.

"I think we'd better come back to the down-stay later," Brenda said. "Let's leash the dogs and try the come-fore." She looked at Lucy. "Why don't you and Hobart follow David and Comanche—although Comanche should probably take lessons from Hobart."

To Lucy's surprise, the boy, David, didn't seem the least bit insulted. In fact, he was grinning wide enough to show two dimples.

"What's the come-fore?" Lucy asked him.

"It's pretty easy, even for this renegade." He patted Comanche. "Just do what we do." Lucy watched as David had the dog sit and stay. He walked as far away as the leash would allow and called, "Comanche, come-fore!" Comanche trotted over, made a half turn so he was facing the same direction as David, and sat by his master's side.

"I'm glad you came today," David told Lucy, when she and Hobart had executed the manuever. "I've been the only teenager in the class since Tim moved and left Hobart."

Lucy did a double take. "You knew Hobie's old raiser?"

"Yep. Since kindergarten. Tim moved to Florida last month, right after eighth grade. I guess I felt as bad as Hobart did." David read the disbelief in Lucy's face. "What's the matter?"

"It's just that I never expected Hobart's last raiser to be a nice person. I mean, I guess he's nice if he was your friend."

"Sure. He still is. Why?"

"Because Hobart's such a . . . a wimp! He's practically afraid to breathe unless you tell him it's okay. I figured he'd been living with dog abusers before."

David laughed. "Hobart was just born polite. He's a great dog. Listens better than any I've seen. He just needs a little more confidence. Before Tim left, he was working on it. He was really worried that when he moved, Hobart would backslide."

"Well, you can tell him he was right." Lucy stopped talking as Brenda dragged a long, cloth-covered tunnel into the middle of the room. It reminded Lucy of the caterpillar ride at the amusement park.

"Okay, raisers, it's fun time," Brenda called. "The idea is for you to be at one side of this thing and your dog to be at the other. When it's your turn, call your dog to come to you through the tunnel." She grinned at the group. "Sounds simple, doesn't it?"

Sure, if you didn't mind feeling like you'd been trapped in a pitch-black hole, Lucy thought. She'd always hated the caterpillar ride. It was dark and close and hard to breathe in there. She'd never been one hundred percent certain that she'd be let out again. But the ride was Anna's favorite, so whenever their father took them to the amusement park, Lucy had to go on it anyway. Otherwise, Anna would refuse to accompany her on the Tilt-a-Whirl, which was Lucy's favorite.

"George, why don't you and Lily go first?" Brenda said.

George had a thin pouf of white hair on his head and pale skin that was blotched with pink. Below his baby-blue T-shirt, his arms were surprisingly muscled. Lucy wondered if he was the sexy senior citizen's husband.

George bent down and peered into the tunnel. "Lily, come!"

Lily walked halfway through the tunnel—and sat down.

"Lily, come here!"

Lily just sat.

Lucy covered her mouth with a hand. When she met David's eyes, he raised his eyebrows.

George got down on all fours and crawled into the mouth of the tunnel. Then he barked.

Lily jumped up and ran out the way she'd come in.

Lucy couldn't remember the last time she'd laughed so hard. It was amazing how different canine personalities could be! A yellow Lab sashayed into the tunnel and liked it so much, it decided to stay. Its raiser had to coax it out with a breath mint, since another dog had found the emergency supply of biscuits and eaten them all before anyone noticed. Then, a cautious German shepherd crawled through on its belly. It looked like it was doing a bad imitation of a dachshund.

"Well, here goes," David said when it was Comanche's turn. He left the golden retriever wagging its tail and crouched down at the other end of the tunnel. "Comanche, come!" he called. Comanche took off like a cannonball, shooting through the tunnel and running David over.

Lucy wondered if a guide dog could have too much confidence. Her mother seemed to think people could. Once, Lucy's father had insisted they all go for a ride on his friend's motorboat, even though the weatherman was predicting a storm. When her mother had protested, he'd teased, "Come on, Lainie, don't be such a party pooper. The weatherman's just a worrywart. It's what he gets paid for."

And he'd been right! It hadn't rained a single drop. Lucy never understood why that made her mother mad. After they were safely on shore, she'd turned to her husband and snapped. "You're so cocky, you think you're right about everything! One day your luck will turn, Daniel. When it does, I just hope you're the only one who gets hurt!" Then she'd stalked off to wait in the car.

To Lucy, the words had sounded like a prediction. A curse. What if her father's luck turned now, while he was camping in the outback? Would her mother be sorry? Of course, whatever happened—scorpions, crocodiles, headhunters—wouldn't be her mother's fault. Nothing was anyone's fault. Each of her parents had made sure to tell her this again and again. These things just happen sometimes, they'd said. People change. Mistakes are made.

"Okay, Lucy, your turn," Brenda called. Lucy left Hobart waiting at one end of the tunnel and hurried to the other end. When she bent down and peered through the opening, Hobart was waiting patiently. "Hobart, come!"

Hobart whined. He twitched his feet. He didn't move.

"Hobart, come!" Lucy called again.

Hobart took a step backward.

"Crawl in a little way," Brenda suggested. "Let him see there's nothing to be afraid of."

Lucy got down on her hands and knees. The air inside the tunnel was heavy, and the canvas smelled like a combination of dogs and mildew. She had to swallow to keep herself from gagging. "Hobart, come on! Hurry!" she ordered.

The dog lay down in front of the entrance. His mournful eyes made Lucy wish her arms were long enough to reach out and hug him.

Brenda poked her head in above him. "I guess he's not ready. But don't worry, he probably just needs more time. You can try again next week."

"Sure," Lucy agreed. She was not going to waste her time worrying. She was going to take action! Already she had an idea. She couldn't wait to talk to Cal about it.

FAMILY REUNION

Wet welcome kisses and warm soft bodies
Cousin Buddy's grown leggy
and Cousin Dot's teeth are still crooked
from all our tug-o-war games
Mom serves snacks that quiver the nose
Uncle Swifty gobbles them up
While Aunt Goldie, the natural blonde, flirts
Baby Coco dampens the carpet

Time for games! Dad barks
He's a natural at having fun
Everyone loves him so
all join in a game of tackle
all sing a howling good song
Bony feast! Everybody heel!
Good night! Good night!

Cal eyed the collection of boxes piled on the lawn. "Maybe we should've rounded up a few extras. Mrs. Schaeffer said there are probably some empties down in her basement."

"More? We already have enough cartons here to link Hawaii to Alaska. The tunnel Brenda used was only fourteen feet long." Lucy finished opening a carton and held it up so it framed her face like a TV screen. "Good morning, do-it-yourselfers. Welcome to 'This Old Doghouse.' Today we will show you how to make your dog the perfect tunnel out of a material that's both cheap and recyclable—the cardboard box. Tell the folks at home how we're going to fasten all these boxes together, Carpenter Cal."

Cal pried open another carton and held it up. "Simple, Laborer Lucy. First, we'll open up both the tops and bottoms and tape their flaps upright to make them deeper. I'm using green floral tape, which was donated by my employer, Schaeffer Socials—where every party is a dream come true. But you can use masking or electrical tape or any other sturdy kind. Then I'm going to use my staple gun to attach the cartons to each other in one extra-long row."

"Did you say gun? This is supposed to be a nonviolent show!" Lucy put down her carton and crawled across the grass to scratch Hobart behind the ears. "We'll have this together in no time, Hobie. Then you can practice crawling through. By the next class, you'll be a champion tunneler."

Hobart rolled on his back and offered Lucy his belly for more scratching. He didn't seem particularly anxious to begin his tunneling lessons.

"Quit yakking and hold these two together like this," Cal grumbled. "I can't do everything."

Lucy took the cartons from him. "Did you borrow that staple gun from Mrs. Schaeffer?"

"Nope, it's my mom's. She's got all sorts of tools. Mostly, she uses them at Curl Up and Dye. You know, to unclog the drains, saw off the customers' split ends—stuff like that." Cal's face grew red as he forced the staples through the double thickness of the cardboard.

"The tools at home belong to my dad," Lucy said. "He left them in the garage, but my mom never even looks at them. If something breaks, she leaves it that way. There's a spoon permanently stuck in the garbage disposal."

If she could take a walk inside herself, Lucy imagined, it would be the same. Little things on the blink everywhere. One night, an onset of cramps had caused her to leave the dinner table without eating. When lying down didn't help, she'd written a poem:

SERVICE CALL
I found an ad in the Yellow Pages:
"Home Repairs—We fix anything"
So I called and said
it might be an emergency
A man in a gray uniform rushed to the door
This looks very serious, he frowned
making his rounds
taking notes on a clipboard
sighing tsking sounds
His cap sat on his head like a dead duck's bill
flapping as he spoke
I'm afraid there's no cure for what this house has
  got
Termites? I asked. Dry rot?
Memories, he told me straight out
Spread to every floorboard sill and rail
There's no way to operate, it's gone too far
I'm sorry
We hung our heads a moment
I think he was praying
But I was smiling inside
And when he left, I sat down to have
a glass of milk and remember

Cal stapled another carton onto the lineup. "My mom is pretty handy. She calls it being self-sufficient. She says I take after her that way."

Lucy sat back on the grass. "I don't really take after anyone."

"I thought your father was a writer."

"He writes advertising. It's a totally different thing from poetry." Lucy grabbed another carton and held it in place.

Cal squeezed the stapler with sudden force. "I wish I knew if something about me *wasn't* like my father. I'd even settle for knowing something about me that *was* like him."

Lucy pulled up a fistful of grass. She and Cal had been neighbors and friends since they'd been toddlers. He'd *always* lived alone with his mom. She'd never imagined it any other way. How could she? No man ever came to take him out on Sundays. He didn't bring an overstuffed duffel bag to school on alternating Fridays, like some of the kids from divorced families that she knew. He didn't even get letters from faraway places. And he'd never acted like it bothered him.

"Did you ever see your father?"

"Nope."

"Not even in a picture."

"Uh-uh. My mom always says I was a wonderful accident. Like a hit-and-run. She hardly saw the guy that struck her, but she got a million-dollar settlement— me." Cal looked up and grinned.

It wasn't a real smile, Lucy knew. She wanted to put

her hand over his mouth and wipe it away. Instead, she opened her fist and let the grass trickle out like green rain. "Maybe you could try to find him."

Cal shrugged. "Sometimes I dream about it. But when I wake up I ask myself, why? He has no idea that I exist. He never meant to have me. That's not what being a father is about."

"Yeah, I guess," Lucy said, but she wasn't convinced he was right. Cal's father hadn't ever been given a chance. If someone told him he had a kid, he might care after all. It was different from giving up your kids after you'd lived with them. That was worse.

By the time they'd tacked on the last carton, the tunnel stretched halfway across the yard. Lucy stood up and surveyed their work. "It's going to be dark inside," she said.

"I could cut a window in it. Or a skylight. I've got a box cutter, too." Cal held up the tool.

"But that would make it less like Brenda's. There's no light in hers, either."

"Maybe that's the problem."

A stanza from a poem by Emily Dickinson popped up in Lucy's head.

> *Either the Darkness alters—*
> *Or something in the sight*
> *Adjusts itself to Midnight—*
> *And Life steps almost straight.*

She knew the words weren't really about nighttime darkness. They were about the kind of darkness that could be inside a person. She felt as if Emily were trying to tell her something. Be brave? Learn to adjust? Quit whining and straighten up? She yanked up another handful of grass from the lawn.

"Lucy—what about the window?"

"Go ahead. Make one."

Cal cut a rectangle about midway along the tunnel. Then he began stapling a red ribbon across the entrance. Lucy recognized it as a scrap from the bows they'd been tying at Mrs. Schaeffer's earlier.

"What's that for?"

"The opening ceremony. They do it for all new tunnels and bridges. You have to cut a ribbon to make it official." Cal held up scissors, but when Lucy reached for them he drew them back. "First you have to give it a name."

Most of the tunnels and bridges Lucy knew were named for Revolutionary War heroes. She wondered how George Washington would feel about having his name on a chain of cardboard boxes that had once held cereal and toilet paper. "Ummm, how about just calling it The Caterpillar?"

"Hey, that's pretty good! A creature with a destiny. Ordinary today, but awesome tomorrow. Just like Hobart." Cal handed her the scissors.

Lucy snipped the ribbon. When Cal applauded, Hobart looked up and wagged his tail.

"Okay, time to try it out. Stay, Hobie." Lucy bounded down to the other end and peeked inside. "Hobart, come!" she called.

Nothing happened. Lucy looked around the side. "He's still here," Cal announced.

"I can see that. Let's try it again. This time give his rear end a little push." Lucy bent down in front of the tunnel. "Hobart, come! Come on, boy!"

Hobart didn't move.

"Did you push him?" Lucy peered around the side again.

"I think he's upset or something. He looks all droopy. Maybe you ought to crawl in from this end and let him follow you."

Lucy straightened up and kicked at the tunnel. "This is ridiculous! What's wrong with you, Hobart? This thing's just a bunch of old cartons."

Cal rubbed the dog's head. "Take it easy. Maybe he's claustrophobic. He might have gotten trapped in a closet when he was a puppy. Why don't you take a dog biscuit in there with you?" He reached into the box he'd insisted on bringing along.

Lucy sighed loudly, but she came around and took the biscuit. Then she wiggled in backward and held it out. "Hobart, look! Want it? Then come here."

Hobart took one step. And another.

Lucy wriggled backward a bit further. "That's right, Hobie, you can do it," she crooned. "Come!"

Hobart stood stiffly, not moving except for his

tongue, which flapped in rhythm to his quick, panicky breaths. Suddenly, the scratchy cardboard and the hot, doggy air were more than Lucy could stand. "Give him a push, Cal!" she ordered.

"I don't think we ought to."

"Just do it! Once he sees it's safe, he'll come on his own."

"I can't."

"Then I'll pull him!" Slowly, Lucy began creeping toward the dog. As if he understood her plan, the whites of Hobie's eyes grew large. He backed out stumbling over his own legs and slunk behind Cal.

Lucy came tearing out of the tunnel, battering the sides and ripping the last carton. "We almost got him in there! Why didn't you push him when you had the chance?"

"I'm not so mean," Cal mumbled.

"You think I'm mean?"

"No, you're impatient. But it's making you want to do something mean."

"I just wanted you to give him a little push! I didn't ask you to hit him."

Cal stroked Hobie's back. The dog groaned softly and laid his head in Cal's lap. "Did you ever dive off the board at the town pool, Lucy?"

"You know I didn't!"

"Why?"

Lucy snorted. Cal already knew the answer. But he was waiting for her to say it.

"Because I'm afraid."

Cal nodded. "Do you think if I pushed you off, you'd do it on your own next time?"

Lucy felt a dangerous bubbling inside, like she'd somehow swallowed that geyser in Yellowstone Park—Old Faithful. "Why don't you just shut up for once!"

"Hobie's got to overcome his fear on his own, Lu."

"Shut up! Shut up! Shut up!" Lucy was on her feet, shouting. "You're so cocky, you think you're right about everything!" A strand of her hair flew into her mouth. It tasted surprisingly salty, like it had been blown about in a strong sea wind. She dropped in a heap on the grass.

"Lu, are you okay?"

Lucy shrugged.

"Look, I'm sorry," Cal said. "I don't know anything about dog training. I should have kept my mouth shut."

"It's not that." Lucy's smile looked more like a wince. "You know what we were doing just now?"

"No, what?"

"Arguing like parents over what's best for our kid."

"We were?"

"Believe me, I know."

"Wow, weird!" Cal flopped onto his back.

It was so quiet, Lucy could hear the bees buzzing in the mock orange bush. Honeybees didn't have parents, she knew. The queen laid all the eggs for the colony, but once they hatched, the babies were raised in a kind of bee nursery by bee nursemaids. There was no arguing over what the baby bees should eat or how late they could stay up. No one's feelings got hurt. Bees didn't have feelings anyway. The drones that fertilized the queen bee's eggs—like fathers—were allowed to starve to death after they were no longer of use.

"You really think I was acting like a father?" Cal asked after a while.

Lucy shrugged. "A little."

A smile stretched across Cal's face. He reached in the biscuit box and handed another one to Hobart. "Here, boy. You look hungry. Come to think of it, I'm starved." He turned to Lucy. "You want to get some pizza?"

"I'm not hungry. Anyway, I want to finish a poem." Lucy stood up and brushed herself off. She was relieved when Hobie sprang up, ready to follow. "Want to help me try The Caterpillar again tomorrow?"

"Sure." Cal watched Lucy lope toward the house with Hobart following at her heels. Just before she disappeared inside, he shouted, "Hey! Take good care of my kid."

12

"Here's some extra cash for soda and ice cream," Mrs. Rising said, holding three five-dollar bills. "There's not a lot of shade at the fairgrounds, and they're predicting a really hot day."

Lucy looked at the offering. Fifteen dollars seemed like a lot of money for soda and ice cream, especially after the big scene last year over how much sweet stuff she'd consumed. She wondered if her mother was sorry now or if she just wanted to ensure that Lucy would have a good time today.

"Thanks." Lucy took the money and tucked it into her shorts pocket. "I'm going to drop Hobie at the Parkers'. Cal's going to bring him along to swim practice. He says there's a shady place nearby where he can tie Hobie up."

"That's nice. Tell Cal he can bring Hobart back here after four. I should be home by then."

"Where are you going?"

Mrs. Rising turned to the sink and began poking in the garbage disposal with a pliers. "Just to the library. I promised to help the father of one of my campers pick out some storybooks about children with disabilities. His daughter, Danielle, has spina bifida. She wears braces on both legs." She leaned further into the sink. "Afterward we're going out to lunch."

"You are?"

"Yes. We'll probably take Dani to McDonald's. She's seven and loves cheeseburgers."

"Oh." Lucy wondered why her heart was beating so fast. Her mother was only going out with one of her campers and her father. It was no big deal. It wasn't like a date. After all, her mother was a librarian. It was her job to help people find books. But why wasn't the kid's mother going along? Of course, she might work on Saturdays. Or perhaps she had to stay home and take care of a baby. Or maybe she and her husband were divorced.

Lucy wondered if she should drop her father a little warning. *Dear Dad, I thought I'd send you a note since I'm all alone today. Anna's out with Jeremy and Mom's having lunch with Mr. X . . .* That might make her father jealous—which wouldn't necessarily be a bad thing. Maybe he'd realize that he still cared about his wife. Maybe he'd even take the next flight home. Lucy hoped her mother would be wearing her tight black shorts and her camp T-shirt when her father came through the door. She looked great in those. Danielle's father had probably noticed that, too. Maybe, when she sent the letter, Lucy could even include a photo of her mother wearing that outfit. She wondered if she should pretend she was feeling sick so she could stay home and write to her father today. Then she remembered that she couldn't send him a letter now, even if she wanted to. He was hiking through the outback. She didn't even know when he'd return.

"I got it!" Lucy's mother spun around, arm raised in triumph. In her hand were the pliers, their jaws closed around a spoon.

Lucy got into the log flume boat and gripped the siderails. The hollowed-out log rocked back and forth as Jeremy plunked down behind her. When they'd found out only two people could fit in each boat, Lucy and Anna had sat together the first time, while Jeremy watched and waved. Now that it was his turn, Jeremy had asked Lucy to ride with him. Lucy was surprised, but she didn't resist. She didn't mind keeping Anna and Jeremy apart.

"Who's your favorite poet?" Jeremy asked, while they waited for the ride to begin.

Lucy looked into the narrow channel of water. "Emily Dickinson."

"Really? You know, I heard this amazing thing about Dickinson in class this year. Practically all of her poems can be sung to the tune of 'The Yellow Rose of Texas'!"

Lucy stared at him blankly.

"No, really! Listen to this!" Jeremy closed his eyes and tapped his foot against the inside of the boat. "For

each ecstatic instant . . . We must an anguish pay . . .
In keen and quivering ratio . . . To the ecstasy . . ."

Lucy recognized the tune as one played by school marching bands at parades and football games. She thought of girls in short fringed skirts, white cowboy hats, and western boots, marching as they sang. She wanted to jump out of the log boat, but it had already begun its slow climb up the first hill.

"Listen to this one," Jeremy continued. "The brain is wider than the Sky . . . For put them side by side . . . The one the other will contain . . . With ease and You beside . . ."

As the boat approached the crest of the hill, Lucy began screaming.

"Hey, the first hill's only a little one," Jeremy complained. "What are you going to do after you've broken the sound barrier?"

Anna met them at the exit to the log flume. "It looked like you were doing a lot more yelling the second time around, Lu," she teased. Then she and Jeremy kissed as if they'd been separated for days.

"I'm going to the bathroom," Lucy said.

"Okay, we'll meet you over by the sheep pen. They let you feed the lambs with bottles. They're so sweet!"

Lambs, Lucy knew, were one of Australia's leading farm products. She used to love lamb chops until she was old enough to realize their name actually meant something. Then her mother had to stop serving them because Lucy would cry through dinner, even if she was only eating peanut butter and jelly.

Did other people think the same way? Maybe they just were better at hiding their feelings. Sometimes Lucy wished she could curl up in the brains of strangers so she could see what they felt. To know whether they, too, had tiny weather systems passing behind their eyes, bringing storms without warning.

She walked across the dusty field toward the restrooms. All around her, families talked and laughed. Some of the parents looked like they weren't any older than Anna and Jeremy. Anna would get married someday, too. Anna was lovable.

Lucy wasn't planning to ever get married. She was going to be independent. A famous poet. She thought she might like to live in the woods. She'd have a special friend like Cal who knew a lot about nature. Cal would be perfect himself, except for the fact that he wanted to get married. Cal was lovable.

At least she could have a dog. They weren't fussy about who they attached themselves to. Look at Hobie. He sat by her feet and slept by her bed. He did whatever she asked (well, almost). He followed her around as if he were in love. When she was going out without him, he lay by the door as if his heart were breaking.

Lucy pushed through the bathroom door and locked

herself into a stall. Once Hobie was placed with a blind person, he would be fine. Brenda had assured her that dogs of his breed changed owners easily. And her mother had promised that they would get another dog. If Hobie could bond with another person, Lucy should be able to love another dog. Shouldn't she?

The sun seemed lower in the sky when Lucy stepped out of the restroom. From a distance, she could see that the sheep pen was empty. She was anxious to go home. She wanted to see if Cal had gotten Hobie to go through the tunnel. And if her mother was back from McDonald's. She hadn't mentioned her mother's outing to Anna. She wondered if her sister knew.

She scanned the horizon, looking for Anna. She didn't have to look far. Anna and Jeremy were lying in each other's arms under the tree where they'd had lunch. The hot dogs and soda in Lucy's stomach threatened to reappear. She turned around and headed for the refreshment stand.

"A giant Coke, please," she said when it was her turn. She paid for the drink and gulped down the soda as fast as she could. The sweetness made the back of her throat ache, and the fizz made her stomach feel like exploding into a thousand pieces.

"Lucy, there you are!" she heard Anna say behind her. "We were worried about you."

Lucy whirled around to say "I bet." Instead, she threw up.

REMEDIAL LIFE

In nursery school I heard
nothing can stop the Big Bad Wolf
if he wants to come through your door.

In Sunday school I learned
if the rains come
nothing will keep you ashore.

On TV I saw
the cyclone blow Dorothy to Oz
where all was green.

Later on the news I saw
people blown to smithereens—
not by wind or water,
it was guns and AIDS and war.

You'd think by now
I would have learned
when darkness bumps the door
you might as well invite it in
and let its ghostly work begin

13

"Lucy? I saw your light on. Can I come in?"

Lucy glanced at her clock. It was two A.M. She clicked the little box that made The Great Eye's screen go blue and wordless. "Okay."

But Anna stayed in the doorway. "Are you writing a poem?"

"Yes."

"Can I read it?"

"No—not yet. It's not any good."

Hobart had been sleeping beside Lucy's chair. Without getting up, he wagged his tail at Anna. His mouth opened in a wide yawn and closed with an almost-human groan.

Anna laughed and bent down to pet him. "I couldn't sleep and then I remembered Jeremy got you something at the fair."

"I don't need anything."

"You mean you don't *want* anything." Anna closed the door and leaned against it. "I was hoping you'd get to like him a little today."

"He thinks Emily Dickinson wrote country-and-western songs." Lucy didn't try to disguise the disdain in her voice. "Anyway, he's *your* boyfriend. Why do I have to like him?"

"Because I do. You would, too, if you'd give him a chance. Jeremy understands what's happened to us. In a way, he knows what it's like."

"Sure."

Anna closed her eyes. "Oh, Lucy, you're not the only one in the world who's ever had anything bad happen to them. I'm going to let you in on something Jeremy shared with me. It's very private, but I think he'd understand why I'm telling you now."

Lucy clasped her hands together to keep them from flying up to cover her ears. When she was younger, everyone she knew was safe and happy. Now there were missing fathers and mothers and children everywhere. Even the dog had lost someone. She stared at the blank computer screen. She wished it would open up and let her inside.

"When he was almost two, Jeremy was adopted." Anna's voice was quiet but insistent. "For the first few weeks, when his new parents tried to put him to bed at night, he screamed and screamed. He couldn't talk. His folks didn't know what to do.

"One night, when he saw them coming to get him, he ran into their room. He picked up their shoes and wouldn't let go. Somehow they figured they ought to let him take those shoes into his crib. And Jeremy went right to sleep. Every night, after that, he collected their shoes at bedtime. He threw them into the crib himself."

"Maybe he was afraid they would leave in the middle of the night," Lucy said. "He might have figured they couldn't go anywhere without shoes."

"Right. But here's what happened. After Jeremy was asleep, his parents always sneaked back to check on him. One night, after about two months, they came in and found their shoes in the middle of the floor."

"He'd thrown them out of the crib?"

"Yes. His parents woke him up and danced him all around the house. They knew he finally trusted them."

Lucy tried to ignore the image shaping itself in her mind like a new poem. A tiny boy with an armload of shoes. She didn't want to shed any tears over Jeremy. Why was Anna telling her this? To show that they had something in common? Maybe they did. They were all losers.

Anna pulled something red out of the pocket of her robe. "Jeremy bought this for you today. While you were in the restroom."

"A bandana?"

"His collie, Pat, used to wear one. Jeremy read that wearing a bandana can raise a dog's sense of self-esteem. He thinks it might help Hobart."

"Jeremy's a dog psychologist? Give me a break."

Anna dropped the bandana onto Lucy's bed. "Look, you don't have to believe it. But if you're going to put it on him, Jeremy says you should sleep with it first, so it has your scent."

Lucy ran her fingers lightly over The Great Eye's keyboard.

"I'll let you get back to your poem now," Anna said, but she was still leaning against the door. She examined the tie of her bathrobe for a few seconds, then cleared her throat. "You know it's funny we haven't heard from Dad lately."

Lucy looked away. "There aren't any mailboxes where he is now."

"What do you mean?"

"Dad's off exploring the outback. If he hasn't been eaten by a crocodile yet. Or stung by a deadly scorpion. Or attacked by headhunters." It was strange how much pleasure Lucy suddenly felt, laying out the grisly possibilities for her sister.

"You got a letter?"

Lucy gave a single nod. The word *smug* entered her mind. It was an ugly word, exactly right for how she felt. She'd wanted Anna to feel hurt. Pain was something they could still share.

But when Anna finally spoke, her voice was as cold as their day on Turtle Shell Pond. "If I got a letter, I'd tell you, Lucy. I wouldn't be so selfish. What did you do, eat it?" She didn't wait for an answer. And she didn't look back as she opened the door and walked out without closing it behind her.

Lucy waited until she heard her sister's feet retreat down the hall. Then she opened the top drawer of her desk and reached all the way in the back. The half-a-letter was still there. She gave it a pat and closed the drawer.

When she looked up, The Great Eye was staring at her. Lucy avoided its blue gaze as she switched it off. She picked up the crumpled bandana from her mattress and folded it into a small, perfect square. Then she tucked it under her pillow.

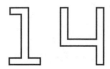

As she came downstairs, Lucy could hear her mother and sister, their voices rising and falling like the perking of the coffeepot. It was this way every morning now. Yet just last summer, Anna had slept late like Lucy. When they had finally ambled into the kitchen together, their mother was already off doing errands or visiting friends.

"Morning, honey," Mrs. Rising said in a hearty voice. "Hey, Hobart looks pretty cute in that bandana. Where'd it come from?"

"Jeremy." As she slipped into a chair, Lucy snuck a glance at her sister. Anna's eyes swept over Hobart, but she didn't smile.

"You can take the car, Anna," Mrs. Rising said as she popped more bread into the toaster. "Rick Stern— Dani's father—has offered to drive me to camp. He says our house is on his way."

"You mean I'm going to have wheels for the rest of the summer?"

"Until camp is over."

"Wow! I can't wait to tell Jeremy he doesn't have to pick me up anymore. Gas is costing him a fortune!"

"Well, now it's going to cost *you* a fortune," Mrs. Rising said. "Just be sure you're back in time for an early dinner. Lucy and Hobart have class tonight." She turned to Lucy. "Right, Lu?"

Lucy barely nodded. All she could think of was her mother in the Sterns' car. Five days a week. Probably her mother would sit up front with Mr. Stern—Rick—and Dani would sit in the back. They might play the radio. Her mother liked the golden oldies, corny love songs with names like "You've Lost That Lovin' Feeling" and "A Groovy Kind of Love." She always sang along. Probably she'd encourage Dani to join in, too. And on the way home, her mother might sing the same silly songs she'd sung to Lucy when she was small, "Little Rabbit Foo Foo" and "Bingo Was His Name-O," until Dani fell asleep. Then Rick and Lainie would be alone together.

Lucy had to work hard to swallow the toast in her mouth. "I'll make dinner tonight, Mom. It's my fault we have to eat early."

"That would be really nice. I was planning on hamburgers. All you have to do is shape them and put them in the broiler at quarter to six."

"Can I season them any way I want?"

Mrs. Rising and Anna both looked at Lucy. "What way?" they asked at the same time.

Lucy made her voice light, teasing. "Does McDonald's tell Burger King its secrets?"

"There'd better not be anything in my burger I don't recognize," Anna warned.

"Don't worry, I'll give you exactly what you want," Lucy said seriously. But she couldn't keep from smiling.

Cal was already at the workbench when Lucy opened her neighbor's back door. "Hi, where's Mrs. Schaeffer?" she asked as Hobart scooted by her, butting his head into Cal's knees.

"Downtown at the flower market. She's low on ferns." Cal scratched the dog's ears. "Hey, buddy! You forgot to take this home with you yesterday." He held up a red plastic Frisbee.

"Where'd you get that?" Lucy was trying not to notice the enthusiastic greeting Hobart was giving Cal. His entire rear end was wagging. She wished he would stop already.

"In town yesterday. When I couldn't even get him to go *near* the tunnel, I figured a game might loosen him up. You wouldn't believe what a great catcher he is— even if my idea bombed."

As if to demonstrate his skill, Hobart took the Frisbee gently in his teeth and brought it over to Lucy. She gave him an extra-big hug. "Good dog! When I've finished working, we'll have a game," she promised. She surveyed the thick white sheet of foam core on the tabletop. The words *Mike and Angie* had been penciled on it in big, chunky letters. "What's this?"

"A sign for Mike and Angie's surprise engagement party." Cal put a finger to his lips. "Don't tell them."

"Tell them? I don't even know them." Lucy lifted a razor knife lying on the workbench. "Is this for cutting out the letters?"

"Uh-huh. Then we have to spray them with this glitter paint." Cal nodded toward a can with a sparkly gold cap.

Lucy pretended to read the instructions on the can. She wondered if someday she'd be painting *Anna and Jeremy* in sparkly letters. Or *Lainie and Rick*. She put down the can with a thump. "This is going to be the tackiest, most obnoxious decoration in the entire universe."

Cal looked up. "I thought girls liked glittery stuff."

"Not *this* girl."

When the letters were twinkling like newly discovered stars, they left them on the workbench to dry and strolled back to Lucy's yard. Hobart carried the Frisbee in his mouth, but when he saw the tunnel, he dropped it and lay down, refusing to go any closer.

"Oops—he's on to us," Cal said.

Lucy looked at the red Frisbee lying in the grass and then at the long chain of cardboard boxes. "I just had a great idea!"

"What?"

"You'll see." Lucy walked across the grass and

stopped in front of the disc, staring as if she hadn't seen it before. "Oh, look, Cal," she said in a high, dramatic voice, "let's play Frisbee!"

Hobart's ears perked up, but he didn't move.

Cal shot Lucy a quizzical look. "Okay."

Lucy sailed the Frisbee to him. He caught it easily and sent it back. "Don't try anything fancy," Lucy said. "And don't pay any attention to you-know-who." Her eyes slid sideways to indicate Hobart. The dog's head was swiveling back and forth, following the Frisbee. Finally, he leapt up and raced over to Lucy, catching the disc just in front of her.

"That's right, you can play, too," Lucy crooned. "Give it back to me now and I'll throw it for you."

Hobart kept his mouth clamped shut. "Quit it, Hobie!" Lucy tugged at the disc. Hobart tugged back.

"Looks like he wants to play a different game," Cal said. He had a big grin on his face.

Lucy glared at him. She wondered if she was going to have to wait until Hobart ate dinner to get the Frisbee back. Then she remembered the command. "Hobart, leave it!" she ordered.

Hobart gave a small, final tug and opened his mouth.

"Good dog!" Lucy praised him. "Now you get to chase it again. Ready?" She turned to the tunnel and sailed the Frisbee right inside the opening.

Hobart raced after it. "That's right, get it! Get it!" Lucy jumped up and down, clapping.

Like a boxer, Cal's hands were balled into tight fists. "Go, boy, go!" he cheered.

Hobart stopped short in front of the tunnel. With a paw, he tried to reach the Frisbee, but the disc was in too far.

"Go on, you can do it!" Lucy said encouragingly. The dog pawed the ground. He danced back and forth in front of the tunnel, looking at Lucy and Cal with bright, hopeful eyes. He opened his mouth—and let out a loud, deep bark.

The sound reverberated in Lucy's chest like she'd swallowed a tom-tom. "Did you hear that? He barked! I just realized I never heard him bark before!"

Hobart sat down suddenly. He looked to Lucy like he was thinking. Then he barked again. And again and again.

"Well, he's definitely a baritone." Cal had to speak loudly over the racket the dog was making. "Maybe you'd better get it for him before all the houses around here start collapsing."

"Okay, Hobie, okay!" Lucy crawled in and tossed the Frisbee out to him. Hobart caught it and began parading around the yard.

"Well, it was a good idea, anyway," Cal said, as Lucy clambered to her feet.

"Thanks." She wasn't really disappointed. At least

Hobie had developed enough confidence to speak for himself now. And his bark had been big and bold. It was, she thought, the kind of sound only a dog with great courage could make.

Lucy hurried into the kitchen and washed her hands in the sink. Before she'd realized it, the afternoon had slipped away. She wanted to finish preparing the burgers before Anna came home. The hamburger meat was waiting for her in the refrigerator. She took it out of its plastic wrapping and plopped it into a large bowl. From the cupboard, she collected an armload of spices. She didn't know what some of them were, but it didn't matter. Just as long as there were lots of different flavors and textures. She sprinkled in salt, pepper, chili powder, garlic powder, minced onion, oregano, allspice, cumin, cilantro, and coriander. All the while, she thought about what she'd once read in the encyclopedia. In Australia, the Aborigines ate parts of their dead relatives in order to strengthen the ties between dead members of the family and the living ones.

Upstairs, in the back of her desk drawer, Lucy found the remaining half of her father's letter. She carried it down to the kitchen and ripped it into pieces no bigger than the minced onion flakes. Her hand trembled a little as she sprinkled them into the burger mixture. Micro bits of letters that had once been words, sentences, thoughts, and feelings. Her father's. And yet they blended right into the mixture, no different than the spices. Her mother and Anna would never notice them. Lucy knew that paper really didn't have any taste.

She was about to stir in the last few shreds when Hobart nudged the back of her legs with his head.

"Are you a hungry dog?" Lucy asked him. It occurred to her that her father had a lot of confidence. More than enough to spare. If eating his words could strengthen their bonds, could it also strengthen Hobie's spirit? Lucy picked up his dish and brushed the last few bits of letter into it.

15

As soon as they entered the church basement, Hobart pulled Lucy over to David and Comanche. "He sure seems full of energy tonight," David said. "What have you been feeding him—pep pills?"

"Oh, just a secret family recipe—Australian Surprise." Lucy looked down at Hobart. He *was* acting differently, wagging his tail and lunging playfully at Comanche. "I guess he's feeling more relaxed now that he's used to me," she said, trying not to show the burst of pride she felt.

"You're not that hard to get used to," David teased. "You know, I tried to put a bandana like that on Comanche once, but he pulled it right off and started eating it."

"Some people think wearing a bandana raises a dog's sense of self-respect." Lucy couldn't believe she was actually quoting Jeremy! When she got home, she was going to wash her mouth out with soap.

"Really? Well, Comanche's sense of self-respect is probably high enough already. If he could talk, he'd be ordering me around. *'Bring me a biscuit, Dave. Scratch me behind the ear.'* "

Lucy laughed. "I guess he won't have any trouble

passing the confidence part of the test for training school."

"Yeah, I guess not," David said. With his long, bony fingers, he stroked Comanche's head lightly.

"Tonight we're going to watch a video about the training of a guide dog team," Brenda announced when everyone had arrived. "It will show you the kind of life that's in store for your dogs and the people who will get them. I hope you'll find it encouraging."

Sitting on the floor in the darkened room, Lucy rested a hand on Hobart's firm back. He was napping peacefully alongside her, not even caring to preview his future. Lucy had to fight the urge to close her eyes, too. To enjoy the closeness of the moment, without thinking about its end.

The film was about a boy named Rob, a senior in high school who had diabetes. In spite of his condition, Rob appeared to be living a pretty regular life at the beginning of the story. He'd just gotten his driver's license, he was a forward on his school's soccer team (which lost every game that season), and he played the saxophone in a band with his friends. Then Rob began to lose his sight due to a condition called diabetic retinopathy. It wasn't surprising that he dropped off the soccer team or that his car sat in the driveway. But he didn't play the sax either, even though he'd memorized his favorite music. And when his friends came by, he was always too busy for them. Rob spent all his time in his room. Poring over photo albums he would soon be unable to see. Using a magnifier to read books he'd always meant to when he was younger. *Treasure Island, The Wind in the Willows*. Lucy thought of Toad and Mole and dug the heels of her hands in her eyes.

Weeks before graduation, Rob dropped out of school. Most days he stayed in bed. The blankets just seemed too heavy, he explained, making Lucy's breath stop. Then he got Arrow, a two-year-old black Lab, from Guiding Friends. Lucy thought Arrow looked just like Hobie. She even wondered if they were related.

The video showed Rob and Arrow training together. Arrow licking Rob's face in the morning. And Rob taking Arrow outside—at first just to the end of the driveway, later up the block and around the neighborhood. As Rob's confidence in Arrow grew, he was able to enjoy many of his favorite activities again. In the last scene, he played his saxophone with the band while Arrow howled along.

When the film was over, everyone was quiet. Lucy guessed they were all thinking the same thing. In a month or two, photos of Hobie and Comanche and the others would be hanging on the wall of honor in Brenda's office. That was what they were working for— raising dogs to help the people who needed them. It was okay to feel a little sad about saying good-bye to your dog. But you had to root for him to pass. To someone like Rob, a guide dog was a second chance at life.

"Time for exercises," Brenda said, breaking into the silence. "We're going to add a new challenge tonight."

Not another one, Lucy fretted. What if Hobie failed at this one, too? If only Brenda would keep the same routine for a while, maybe Hobart could get comfortable. He was every bit as smart as Arrow—only he was being pushed too fast. If he had more time, Lucy was certain he could succeed at anything.

After the come-fore and the down-stay, Brenda had all the raisers pass their dog to the person on their left and go through the exercises again. "We want the dogs to learn to obey whomever they're with," she explained. "In addition to their masters, guide dogs need to cooperate with other family members, trainers, veterinarians, groomers, handlers, emergency personnel, and so on."

As each dog was passed to her, Lucy gave it the commands. Comanche jumped on her, and Lily licked her. Midnight just ignored everything she said. But she never really stopped watching Hobart. Out of the corner of her eye, she saw him sit, walk, turn, and stay for each person in the group. No one seemed to notice how his tail drooped and his ears lay back slightly, giving him a frightened look. Or how he kept glancing over at Lucy, as if he was making sure she was still there. When he'd finally made it back to her, Lucy gave him a hug. "You're a good dog," she whispered.

Was she just imagining it, or did Hobart lean into her knees as if he didn't want to lose contact again?

"I'll just go get the tunnel," Brenda said, disappearing into the next room.

Lucy's throat was so dry, she could barely swallow. She hadn't noticed how hot the basement was. Hobart searched her face, shuffling nervously on his feet. She brought him over to stand next to David and Comanche, hoping the golden retriever's high spirits would rub off on him.

When it was their turn, Lucy walked Hobart to the front of the tunnel. "You can do it, Hobie," she whispered. "I'll be waiting for you right at the other end." She trudged off without looking back. She could feel Hobart watching her every step of the way.

When she couldn't postpone it any longer, Lucy leaned over and stuck her head into the tunnel. "Hobie, come!" she called brightly.

The dog took a step into the tunnel and paused. In her head, Lucy imagined a rope around his neck. She saw herself begin tugging at its other end.

Hobart took another step. And then a third.

Lucy's dream self pulled with all its might. Real beads of sweat formed on her forearms. "That's right, Hobie! Come!" Her voice sounded shrill in her ears. High and demanding.

Hobart froze.

"Hobie, come on! Hurry!"

In a flash, the dog backed out of the tunnel. He ran

around it until he reached Lucy and jumped on her joyfully, as though they'd been separated for days.

"Well, he's still a great listener," David said, chuckling.

Lucy sighed. "Yeah, but he's got to develop the courage to do this. Otherwise he'll never pass his test for training school."

"Sure he will," David said. "Look at him. Just a couple of weeks ago, all he did was lie there. But tonight he had the guts—and the smarts—to find another way to get to you. I bet soon he'll be tearing through that tunnel like a freight train. There's still some time."

Lucy felt a funny clutch in her stomach. "Yeah," she whispered. "But not much."

16

When Lucy came downstairs the next morning, Anna was dawdling over a bowl of cornflakes. She was still wearing the T-shirt and boxers she'd slept in.

"What's the matter, are you sick?" Lucy poured Hobart's food into his dish. "Where's Mom?"

"She had to leave for work early because Mr. Stern couldn't drive her after all. His company sent him out of town to check out some real estate. They're thinking of moving their headquarters."

"Really? They might be moving?" Lucy turned her back so her sister wouldn't notice her smile. "So now you don't get to drive Mom's car, huh?"

"No—and I don't really care, either. I'm taking a day off. Maybe a few. *Jeremy's mother is such a pain!* Do you know, I actually had to repaint their dining room because she wanted it to be ripe banana and, according to her, the color I'd used looked more like ripe lemon."

"What did Jeremy say?"

"Nothing. He's never bothered by anything Mrs. Hoffman does. Last evening, she asked him to mow the lawn when she knew we were on our way to the movies. And he did! Naturally, we missed the show."

"Maybe Jeremy thinks his family will disown him if he doesn't do exactly as they say," Lucy murmured. The thought hovered like a cloud blocking her personal patch of sunshine. Still, she was dumbfounded at how quickly the Australia burgers were working. Not exactly the way she'd expected, but with the same result. Hobie had found a way *around* the tunnel. David had called him gutsy. Mom wasn't riding with the Sterns. And Anna was ticked off at Jeremy.

"Are you working for Mrs. Schaeffer today?" Anna asked.

"No, tomorrow."

"Then let's go to Turtle Shell Pond for a picnic! It'll be like old times."

Underneath the table, Lucy pinched her thigh to keep herself from grinning. If she acted too enthusiastic, Anna might back off and change her mind. "You mean, we have to eat bugs and weeds?"

"No. You can fix us sandwiches while I go up and shower. You're getting to be a pretty good cook."

In summer, the grass around Turtle Shell Pond got so high, it fell over in clumps, like masses of long, tangled hair. On one side of the pond, a lone bench sat empty, its slats chinked and carved with the initials of couples who had probably broken up long ago. The bench was the only sign that people had ever visited at all. There wasn't even a refuse can to dispose of picnic wrappings.

It was too small a pond for anything but frogs and small fish to call home. Sometimes, on their way somewhere else, a pair of Canadian geese might land. But after a day or two, they'd find the pond was too cramped for a good swim. Or else, they'd realize that the local children, who might have fed them the ends of their sandwiches, frequented the town's official park—the one with swings, a fountain, and a baseball diamond. Then the geese would take off again.

"Mmm, I'm so glad we came," Anna said, as she stretched out on the grass. "It's been ages since I've been here!"

"I know," Lucy agreed. "You missed the wild crocus this year." Beside her, Hobart was stretched out, snapping lazily at the moth circling his nose. He looked longer than Lucy remembered, as if he'd grown recently. She ran her fingers lightly over his coat.

"Remember the day we tried to teach that mockingbird we spotted the tune to 'Bingo Was His Name-O' because you'd read that mockingbirds can mimic the songs of other birds?" Anna asked. "I think we each whistled 'Bingo' a hundred times."

"Yeah. Remember when you had to pee and you squatted right over a red anthill?"

"How could I forget?" Anna rubbed her backside. "Remember when we trekked across the pond, although we weren't sure it was frozen? I was actually frightened! It's funny, considering how small the pond really is. If it had cracked, we'd probably have ended up no more than hip deep. I'm sure we could have walked out."

Lucy sat up on her elbows. "But it *was* dangerous! The pond's way deeper than that!"

"I doubt it. It's much too small."

"No—you're wrong! We could have died that day!" When she saw Anna stiffen, Lucy added in a softer voice, "I come here all the time, so I should know."

Anna shook her head. "You always see just what you want to see. Sometimes I wish I could do that."

Lucy tried to think what her sister meant. Once, her father had taken her on a trip to see the apartment building where he'd grown up. In the stories he'd always told about his childhood, it was a towering fortress with turrets and gates, like a castle. Lucy had been surprised to see it looked like any ordinary apartment building. Red brick. Six floors. Now she wondered if her father had been disappointed to see it after all those years. Was that what memories were—a collection of lies? Hers had always seemed as real as if they were photos in an album.

"Come on, Lucy, let's not argue," Anna urged. "This was supposed to be a fun day. Like we used to have. Please?"

Lucy nodded. She told herself it didn't matter about the pond. The important thing was, Anna had missed their times together. She'd said so! When Lucy turned to her sister, she was able to smile. "Want to eat?"

"Sure. What did you make?"

"Peanut butter and bananas on whole wheat. There wasn't much in the house."

"Peanut butter sounds great to me. Jeremy's mother gives us tuna and tomato every single day. Can you believe she actually cuts the crusts off his sandwich?"

Lucy flopped back in the grass and giggled. "That's really lame!" Hobart scrambled up and began licking her face. Since that first morning when he'd licked her awake, giggling and licking had become linked in his mind. "Anna, quick! Give him a dog biscuit," she squealed as she squirmed.

Anna dug into the bag and handed him one. Then she unwrapped a sandwich. "Mmm. This reminds me of the picnics we used to go on with Mom and Dad. Mom would always read to us after lunch. Then Dad would take us on a hike to search for dinosaur bones or buried treasure." She laughed with pleasure at the thought. "Sometimes I wish I could have those days back—I mean, before the fighting!"

"But we *will* have them back. Soon!" Lucy could scarcely contain herself. This was what she'd been waiting for—the right moment to confide in Anna. She rushed on, explaining breathlessly. "Not that we believe in buried treasure anymore, but we could still be a family again. It's happening already! Mom's not driving with Mr. Stern, after all. And you're getting sick of Jeremy. I have a feeling Dad's going to come home soon, too."

Anna's smile faded. "Lucy, Dad didn't just go to Australia on a vacation."

"I know that!" Lucy said quickly. "He and Mom

were fighting too much. He needed to get away and think. So maybe he could see how to change things. So that *he* could change." She watched her sister fold the waxed paper sheet her sandwich had been wrapped in, as carefully as if it were a favorite shirt. The air was so still, a passing fly seemed to be moving in slow motion.

When Anna finally looked up, her gaze was steady and unblinking. "Dad could have gotten away by moving across town. Haven't you ever wondered why he went all the way to Australia? Or why he's staying at Sarah Markham's?"

"She's his client. H-his friend." But even as Lucy spoke, she understood. All she'd eaten was a bunch of lies. Suddenly, she couldn't bear the humidity. Her skin was sticky and her head felt like it was floating above her body. Everything she could see rippled eerily through waves of heat. She stood up quickly and wobbled on her feet.

"Mom didn't want to tell you, but I thought you should know. Lucy! Where are you going?"

The bottom of the pond was mucky with mud and leaves. Lucy had to drag each sneakered foot forward as she waded in. Her legs felt dead, like the waterlogged tree stumps mired toward the far end. She could hear Hobart whining at the water's edge, but she pushed on, sending the waterbugs skittering before her. When she finally got to the center, she stopped. Below her cutoffs, the pond's tepid water lapped at her bare thighs.

"You were right!" she called in a voice that was choked and reedy. "God, I was so stupid!"

TRANSPLANT
I think I'll put my heart away,
just for a while, if that's okay
Cover it in bubble wrap,
place it in a jar that's capped
or else, I'll find the right size box—
not too big, with several locks
Then store it in the attic loft
You see, it's simply much too soft
to keep inside my fragile chest
and life right now is such a mess
I shall replace it with a rock
because I know, no matter what
a rock can't yearn or feel or ache
and therefore it will keep me safe

17

Lucy went to bed before dinner, complaining that she felt sick. When she awoke the next morning, her stomach really did hurt. She thought about calling Mrs. Schaeffer to say she couldn't come. She was certain Cal could handle the work by himself. But when Hobie began to whine and pull at the sheets, wanting to be walked and fed, Lucy dragged herself up. Downstairs, on the kitchen table, she found a note saying Anna had accompanied her mother to camp to fill in for an absentee counselor and that Mrs. Rising would call later to see how Lucy was feeling. Once Lucy was up, she decided to go to Mrs. Schaeffer's after all. Her head ached from too much sleep, and there wasn't anything else to do. She didn't even feel like writing.

"What kind of a bird has a pink nest, anyway?" Cal grumbled as he uncapped a can of spray paint.

"The same kind that lays the marshmallow eggs that go in them." Lucy spread some newspaper over the grass and lined up the little straw baskets. Mrs. Schaeffer had suggested they work outside, so they wouldn't have to breathe the paint fumes.

"You've got to admit they're going to make interesting centerpieces."

Cal held the spray can at arm's length and aimed it at a basket. "Anything with food in it makes a great centerpiece. If I ever give a party, I'm going to use giant ferns for plates and pile them with edible weeds. That would be really original, not to mention environmentally friendly."

"Well, don't invite me," Lucy said. Once she'd read about a starving girl in the mountains of Montana who ate wild bitterroot to survive. Although Lucy had never traveled further west than Niagara Falls, she was certain she knew how bitterroot tasted. Sharp and prickly, like a mouthful of anger.

With his pinky, Cal flipped the basket over and sprayed the bottom. "For your information, weeds can be very tasty. I saw this great *National Geographic* special about them last night."

"I thought you had a swim competition last night." Lucy took the can and sprayed another basket. A light breeze carried some of the spray onto the lawn and speckled a patch of grass pink.

Cal picked up Hobart's Frisbee and sailed it across the Schaeffers' yard. He watched him catch it before he answered. "I skipped it."

"Were you sick?"

"I just didn't feel like going."

Lucy gave him a sidelong glance. His face looked

like he'd just swallowed a mouthful of wild bitterroot. Something was wrong. Cal had never missed a swim meet that she knew of. "Did you get suspended from the team for fooling around?"

"No. Actually, I'm thinking of quitting."

"Cal! Why?"

With the back of his arm, Cal wiped the sweat off his forehead. "It's too time-consuming. They go out for ice cream after every meet."

Lucy eyed him skeptically. Was Cal on a diet? Perhaps he thought he could swim faster if he took off a few pounds. She watched him spray the four remaining baskets all at once. His aim had become careless, almost wild. There was more paint on the newspaper than on the straw. Inside her head, a scene came slowly into focus, like a Polaroid snapshot developing. "Who goes out?"

"The guys—and their fathers."

"Oh." It was just as Lucy thought. She wished she could tell Cal that if his father had known him, he would never have abandoned him.

"It's no big deal. I could go, too. I just don't want to," Cal said. Hobie came trotting back and pressed the Frisbee into his hand. But Cal ignored him and began collecting the baskets.

"I don't think they're dry," Lucy warned him.

Cal shrugged. When his arms were full, he started toward the house.

"Hey—want to try the tunnel with Hobie and me this afternoon? We've got another class tonight," Lucy called after him.

"Can't. I've got some stuff to do."

"Sure, Renaissance Man," Lucy said, although Cal had already disappeared inside the Schaeffers' door. With Hobie at her heels, she raced home and bounded up the stairs without stopping. She was breathing hard as she flipped on The Great Eye's switch. For an instant, the blue screen looked blurry. Wet almost.

Are you okay, Eye? Lucy typed. You look sad—just like everyone else around here.

Hmhmhmhmhmhmhmhmhmhmhmhmhmhmhmhm hmhmhmhm.

RENAISSANCE MAN
Perchance if we'd met in Renaissance Days,
you'd have painted my portrait with a mink-tail
    brush
or baked me a bubbling wild-boar pie.
I know I'd have written a sonnet for you
in blackberry ink with a pheasant quill pen
about courage, passion, steadfastness,
and swimming . . .
Mayhap I don't know a lot about history,
but I do know something about hearts.
Yours is too good to ever be broken.

Lucy typed in her last edits and started the printer. While it was clicking, she checked out the window to make sure the street below was empty. Her hand caught the sheet just as the printer spat it out, and she stuffed it into an envelope on her way down the stairs. Excited by the bustle, Hobie followed right behind. But Lucy didn't want to take even the few extra seconds needed to put on his collar and leash. "You wait here, Hobie. I'll be right back," she promised. Then she pulled the screen door shut and streaked across the street to Cal's mailbox.

The raisers and dogs were taking a break while Brenda hunted in the equipment room for another "challenge." Lucy and David watched Hobart and Comanche wrestle. Usually, it was Comanche who had the upper hand, jumping on Hobie, nipping teasingly at his neck and ears. But tonight Comanche was wriggling on his back, while Hobart lunged and darted around him.

"Wow! Hobie's certainly becoming cocky," David said. "I don't think you have to worry about him any-more."

Lucy pursed her lips in a skeptical expression. "Let's just see what Brenda's got in store first." But her smile gave her away. She was so proud of Hobie! She was certain he was the most lovable, intelligent, and loyal dog in all of Guiding Friends.

"You think maybe Brenda's going to bring a skateboard out of that closet? I'd like to see Comanche fly across the room on one of those." David laughed at his own joke. "Actually, I'd like to see *Brenda* fly across on one of those!"

Lucy laughed, too, but her smile faded when she saw Brenda pull a small, round trampoline into the center of the room. It was the kind people who lived in cramped quarters could jump up and down on, or even jump rope on, without moving the furniture. Lucy had seen it advertised on TV.

"In case you're wondering, I'm not expecting the dogs to bounce up and down on this," Brenda said. Lucy chuckled along with the other raisers. It was exactly what she had been thinking.

"I just want the dogs to step up, walk across, and step off again," Brenda explained. "In the city, guide dogs deal with sewer grates, manhole covers, potholes, and planks every day. This exercise will help our dogs become more familiar with surface challenges."

The trampoline was only a foot off the ground. Lucy thought it didn't look like much of a challenge at all. She brought Hobie over to the line that was forming. Midnight, Lily, and Comanche were ahead of them.

Midnight walked perkily at the end of his leash and stepped right onto the trampoline. He took a few cautious steps across the springy surface and got down again, head and tail held high. The line of raisers broke into applause. Grace took a jaunty bow. Midnight got so excited, he ran around in circles, chasing his tail.

"Okay, George, you and Lily are next," Brenda said.

Lily practically ran over to the trampoline. Without even hesitating, she got up on the netting and lay down, curling into a cozy ball.

Below his pouf of white hair, George turned bright pink. "I have one of these at home," he explained. "It's Lily's favorite place to sleep." Lily had to be tugged off the trampoline before Comanche could take his turn.

Lucy squatted down and whispered in Hobart's ear. "Okay, boy, watch carefully." She kept her arm around Hobie as David led Comanche over to the trampoline. Comanche sniffed its leatherette edge and stepped up easily. When he felt the center netting sag, he looked down at his feet as if he were surprised, but with David's encouragement, he took the few steps across. After he'd hopped off, he turned to sniff the leatherette edge again. Before David could stop him, he clamped his jaws around it and dragged the trampoline along the floor.

"Comanche, no! Leave it!" David ordered. Comanche shook the trampoline in his teeth. "No! Stop!" David shouted. Comanche swung the trampoline in a circle.

Lucy wanted to laugh, but she knew it would give Hobie the wrong message about bad behavior. Besides,

David's eyelids fluttered as he stood watching. His rangy arms dangled helplessly. She understood how he felt.

"Better get tough, Dave," Brenda said.

David snapped Comanche's leash hard enough to jerk him to attention. It was a technique Brenda had taught the raisers, although Lucy'd never once had to use it on Hobart. Comanche opened his mouth in surprise and dropped the trampoline. While Brenda brought it back to the center of the room, David led Comanche back to the end of the line. Lucy thought they both looked a bit sorry and sheepish.

"Okay, Lucy, go ahead," Brenda said.

Lucy walked Hobart over to the trampoline. "Come on, boy, up!" she said. Hobart stopped short and sniffed the leatherette. Then he tried to pull Lucy around the trampoline.

"No, you have to step up," Lucy told him. "Come on! Up!" She tried to tug him forward by the leash.

Hobart planted his front feet so firmly, his toenails seemed hammered to the floor. He refused to budge. To Lucy's horror, tears welled up in her eyes. *"Hobie, please,"* she whispered.

"You try getting on first, Lucy," Brenda suggested. "Sit in the middle and see if he'll come to you."

"Okay." Still holding Hobart's leash, Lucy got on the trampoline and sat down cross-legged. "Come on, Hobie, come up here," she murmured in a voice that was shaky.

Hobart gave her a long look. He put a paw onto the trampoline, as if he were testing it. Then he sprang up and plopped onto Lucy's lap, wagging his tail furiously. "Good boy!" Lucy whispered. "You did it!" Hobie licked her nose. Lucy squirmed out from under him and the two of them stepped off onto the floor.

"That was terrific, Lucy!" Brenda said. "Hobart responds just wonderfully to you! I can tell you've really gained his trust."

For the rest of the class, Lucy couldn't stop smiling.

Anna was waiting outside in the car. "Hi," she said, when Lucy opened the back door to let Hobart in. "I told Mom I'd pick you up."

"Thanks." Lucy got into the front and buckled her seatbelt. "Hobie did great tonight." She reached into the backseat and patted his head.

"Did he go through the tunnel?"

"No . . . but he walked on one of those mini-trampolines. He was afraid at first, but when I got on, he followed me without even hesitating. Brenda thinks he's doing really well."

"That's super." Anna put her hands on the steering wheel, but she didn't start the car. "We got a letter, Express Delivery. From Dad." She pointed her chin toward an envelope resting on the dashboard. "I didn't want to open it without you."

"You could have. I don't want to see it anyway."

"Oh, Lucy." Anna reached for the letter. Lucy tried

to ignore her, but her eyes kept darting to the envelope as her sister tore it open and pulled out the single sheet of paper.

Dear Anna and Lucy,
I know it's been a long time, but I am finally coming home! I already have my ticket in my jacket pocket. I'll be leaving on Saturday, August 25th, and arriving twenty-two hours later on Sunday, August 26th. I can't wait to see your beautiful faces again.

Love as always,
Dad

"August twenty-sixth. That's just a month away!" Anna exclaimed. "You were right this afternoon! Dad *is* coming home soon. You must be a witch."

Lucy shrugged. She twisted her fingers through her hair. If she told Anna about the Australia burgers, her sister would think she was crazy for sure. "Are you going to tell Mom?" she asked.

"Of course. We have to."

Lucy pretended she hadn't noticed Anna's choice of the word *we*, but it was a sweet victory to her ears. "Do you think Mom will be glad?"

Anna sighed deeply. "I don't know. It might be too late."

Lucy tried not to think about what it would be like to have her father living in the house again. To feel the rough wool of his jacket against her face when he hugged her. To see him close his eyes the way he always did when he took his first sip of morning coffee. To be the first one to the door when he came home at night, bearing stories and jokes and sticks of Big Red gum. She had to remind herself he was no longer the same person she'd thought he was. And now she was no longer the same either.

"Are you glad?" Anna asked.

Once during a lesson, Mr. Frye had explained to the class about searching for the "objective correlative," which was the exact right word to express what you wanted to say in your poem. *Glad* was definitely not the objective correlative for what Lucy was experiencing. Was there a word that meant an earthquake was happening inside yourself? Ripping you apart and creating fissures so deep they seemed to have no bottom? Sending shocks that reached all the way to the little hairs on your skin? "Sometimes I hate Dad," she whispered.

"I know." Anna reached out a tentative hand and began stroking her hair. "When I first found out about Sarah Markham, I felt that way, too. I actually wrote and told him so. I said I'd never forgive what he'd done to Mom and you. Or to me."

Lucy looked up into Anna's face. Her sister's eyes were a sky blue that made her yearn to fly away.

"But I discovered I couldn't stop loving him. I don't know. Maybe you can love someone and still not forgive him. Or maybe I need to give Dad a second chance whether he deserves it or not, because it makes me feel better."

All the time her sister had been away at college, Lucy had imagined Anna absorbed with schoolwork and friends, too busy to think about home and what had happened. But now another scene unfolded in her mind. In her hivelike dorm, Anna had been living among strangers. Just like bees, everyone flitted around with their own roles and purposes. There'd been no one to help comfort Anna. Until she met Jeremy.

Anna fingered the letter in her lap. "You, uh, want to keep this?"

Lucy searched her face. "No, thanks." She flashed her sister a little smile. "I'm not very hungry right now."

Mrs. Rising was making cinnamon iced tea when they arrived home. Anna found three tall glasses, and Lucy popped ice cubes from a tray. The sound of the ice as it cracked made her shut her eyes tightly. She stood before the freezer and let the cold air chill her face.

"Come on, Lucy, you can't drink iced tea without ice," Anna teased from her place at the table. Lucy poured the cubes into a bowl and brought it over. She wondered how Anna could still make jokes. When her mother asked about Hobart's latest accomplishments, she answered with brief, flat replies. But Mrs. Rising didn't seem to notice. She launched into a story about how she'd taught one of her campers to read.

Lucy barely heard her. She was thinking about her father. Wondering how she could sit with him at dinner or join him on the Saturday morning runs they used to take. What could the two of them possibly say to each other that would not be angry or painful—or a lie?

When she couldn't stand it any longer, she blurted out, "Mom? Dad's coming home."

"Yes, I know."

Anna's head snapped up. "You do?"

"He told me over the phone last week, but he asked me not to tell you. He wanted to do it himself."

Her mother's words appeared in Lucy's mind like a sentence on a page. Her father had telephoned? It was funny, but she'd never expected him to call—or thought of calling him. Somehow, Australia had seemed as unreachable as the stars. But of course they had telephones there. Yet he hadn't called her even once. Was it because she'd refused to write? It didn't matter anymore.

"I guess I'd better clear out the garage," she said. "Cal and I stuck the leftover cartons in there when we were building the tunnel. There's not even space for Dad to park his car."

"He won't need a parking space," Mrs. Rising said.

"Why not?"

Her mother pushed her chair back from the table. "Lucy, didn't your father say why he's coming back?"

Lucy stared at her plate.

Mrs. Rising's voice rose higher. "Anna?"

Lucy heard her sister sniffle. What did Anna understand that she had missed?

"Your father has asked me for a divorce. He's coming back to get the legal work done. I'm sorry. He should have told you himself."

18

SILLY PUTTY TIME
Too long—
the pause dividing words
the beat separating hearts
the light years distancing planets
the wait from dark till light

Too short—
the voyage over oceans
the weeks from here till gone
~~the taste of summer~~
~~the secret that we~~

Eye? I think my brain's turned to Silly Putty.
The words are stuck.
Hmhmhmhmh—

Lucy snapped off the power switch and spun around
in her desk chair. Every day she and Cal had tried to
get Hobie to go through the tunnel. She'd been certain
he was on the verge of a breakthrough. But an entire
week had passed and he hadn't even put a paw inside.
He was stuck in time. And time was running out!
What if in class tonight, Brenda gave up on him? What

if she decided he'd never be good enough for training school?

When the telephone rang, Hobie ran over to it. In spite of herself, Lucy smiled. "I know you're smart," she said, as she lifted the receiver. "So why can't you just walk through that ratty old thing?"

"Lu? You got company?" Cal asked.

"No, I was talking to Hobie."

"Ha! Sorry to interrupt you, but I just had an idea about how we can get him to go through the tunnel. I think it might really work!"

"What is it?"

"Meet me in the yard in two minutes."

Cal was already picking at the tunnel with the back of a hammer when Lucy came outside. "Hey! What are you doing?" she asked.

"Taking this thing apart."

"Why?"

With a sudden jerk, Cal pried off a staple. "This morning I was thinking about how I learned to swim. When I was five, I was afraid of the water. So my mom hired Lenny, the lifeguard at the town pool, to give me lessons. The first session, he asked me to put my chin in. Not even my nose. Just dip my chin in and out, in and out. Finally, I got so bored, I stuck my whole face in."

"What happened?"

"I got water up my nose and I choked."

From the shady spot he'd plopped down in, Hobart snorted loudly. Lucy stifled the urge to do the same. Cal didn't even look up. All of his attention was focused on working another staple out of the cardboard. Lucy could see he was working out something else, too.

"So Lenny said, 'Hold on! Let's take it one step at a time.' Then he taught me how to put my nose and mouth in and blow bubbles." Cal sat back on his haunches and grinned at Lucy.

"But Hobie won't take one step!"

"That's because we got the whole thing backward, Lu. We should've started Hobie with one carton." Cal freed the first box from the chain and handed it to her. "Here, try it."

Cal was, Lucy thought, the smartest person she'd ever met. For an instant, she wondered about his father. Perhaps he was a professor at a university or a doctor researching cures for awful diseases. One thing she felt certain about—he had a good heart.

She took the carton from Cal and set it down between herself and Hobart. Then she got on her hands and knees and looked through it. "Come here, Hobie," she said in a voice that was neither worried nor demanding.

Hobart stood and stuck his head in the carton. He looked up at the roof and down at the floor. With four quick steps, he walked through it and sat down next to Lucy. "Good boy!" she praised him. The dog yawned as if it was nothing at all.

Lucy shook her head and grinned. "Calvin Parker, you are amazing! You think we should try putting another one behind it?"

"Nope. Let's just keep doing it until he's really bored. Until *he's* ready for the next step."

By the end of the afternoon, Hobie could go through a three-carton tunnel. It wasn't much longer than Hobie himself, but Lucy was thrilled with his progress. With a little more effort, she was certain he'd be willing to go through thirty cartons—or three hundred. "Wish us luck tonight," she told Cal as she started for the house. "I'll call you as soon as I'm back from class."

"Okay. Good luck!"

When all the raisers had arrived in the church basement, Brenda called them together. "Before we get started, I have an announcement to make," she said, staring down at the paper in her hands. "Due to scheduling problems, we've had to move up final evaluations by two weeks. They've been set for this Saturday."

Lucy and David turned to each other with stunned faces. "Saturday!" David whispered.

"I know." Lucy touched Hobart's head lightly, as if he might not be real. "I was counting on at least two more sessions. I still don't think he's ready."

David shook his head slowly. "I don't know if *I'm* ready."

"Please bring your dogs to the Guiding Friends Center between nine A.M. and twelve noon," Brenda continued in a flat voice. "We'll be keeping the dogs overnight in order to complete both the behavioral and medical portions of the evaluations. Please don't call us to inquire about how your dog is doing. You will be notified as soon as we've made a final decision." Even though she'd finished reading, Brenda kept her eyes on the paper for a more few seconds before she looked up at the group. "If you have any questions, you can see me after class tonight. Now let's get on with our exercises."

When Brenda brought out the tunnel, Lucy felt the confidence she'd gained that afternoon drain away. All she could think about was peering at Hobie's eyes from the opposite end of the long, dark shaft. This would be his last chance.

Lucy led Hobart to the line of raisers and dogs waiting to try the tunnel. She didn't notice who was ahead of her or who was behind. She didn't watch the other dogs try and succeed—or fail. The same familiar verse of Emily Dickinson's poem about darkness ran through her head, over and over until it had no meaning.

> *Either the Darkness alters—*
> *Or something in the sight*
> *Adjusts itself to Midnight—*
> *And Life steps almost straight.*

And then she and Hobart were next. "Stay, Hobie," she whispered in a soft voice she knew Brenda would not approve of. As she headed for the other end of the tunnel, she didn't look back to see if he'd obeyed. Only the knowledge that he was waiting for her kept her moving. When she got there, she breathed deeply and leaned down to look inside. "Hobie, come!" Her voice was slow and wavery, like talking through water.

Hobart answered with a mournful whine.

"Try to sound more convincing. Like you expect him to obey you," Brenda suggested.

Lucy's back stiffened resentfully, but she made her voice harder and more demanding this time. "Hobart, come!"

The dog staggered forward as if he were sleepwalking. His two front paws were in the tunnel.

"That's right, come here now!" Lucy urged. Even though it was summer, her hands felt painfully cold. The ground was oddly slippery, too. She looked around and saw that a dark row of pines had replaced the sides of the tunnel. Beneath her feet, something shone hard and glittery. Turtle Shell Pond! Frozen—but maybe not all the way through. "Hobie, come on! Hurry!" Lucy called. This time her voice was soft and breathy. Scared.

Hobart began walking through the tunnel. Halfway, his walk turned into a trot. And then a run. He didn't stop until he reached the other side. As Lucy hugged him, the other raisers clapped and cheered. Hobart wagged his tail and barked as if he were cheering, too.

David and Comanche came bounding over. "Hobie,

you did it!" David said, patting the dog on the back. "Tonight you are truly a lionhearted Labrador!" Hobart's entire body wriggled joyfully.

Lucy looked up at David and smiled. For the first time she had the sense they were all part of a team. Raising the dogs was a group effort. Everyone here really cared about one another's success. They deserved to feel proud of Hobart, too. She held Hobie even tighter, feeling she could hug them all.

POEM FOR A LIONHEARTED LABRADOR
It's easy to know Courage
when you see it on TV:
Soldiers fighting unseen enemies
Firemen braving burning buildings
Policemen searching darkened alleys
Grandmas chasing pocketbook snatchers

But there's another kind of courage
that's kind of hard to see:
Going to school on a bad hair day
Admitting you liked reading *Call of the Wild*
Saying you're sorry
Saying good-bye
Crossing the distance from your head to your heart
Finding it's not so far

The doorbell was ringing when Lucy stepped out of the shower. She toweled her shoulders and arms, waiting for someone else to answer. When the bell rang again, she listened for movement on the stairs. There was none. Her sister, she guessed, was on the phone with Jeremy. He'd called right after dinner, and Anna was still talking when Lucy had returned from obedience class. Those two were acting like they'd been separated for a year, instead of a week.

Lucy cracked open the bathroom door and peered down the hall. Her parents'—her mother's—bedroom door was closed. Lucy knew it was Mrs. Rising's way of saying she did not want to be disturbed unless there was a fire, or an earthquake, or a flying saucer landing on their driveway. When the bell rang a third time, Lucy slipped on her terry robe and thumped downstairs. Hobie trailed behind her.

"My mom told me you phoned earlier," Cal said, when she opened the door. "I've been trying to call, but your line's been busy for hours. What's up?"

"Hobart went through the tunnel tonight. He flew through! I wanted you to be the first to know."

"Really? That's awesome!"

"Yeah. I wish you could've been there—you've helped

him so much." Lucy raked her fingers through her wet hair. She wished she'd had time to comb it. "Want to come in and celebrate? We've got ice cream and a raspberry pie my mom and her campers made today."

"Actually, I just had ice cream," Cal said.

"Is that why you weren't home before?"

"Sort of. I went to a swim meet. The ice cream came afterward."

"I thought you dropped off the team!"

"You didn't think the Renaissance Man was really going to give up swimming, did you?" Cal began fiddling with his watchband. He had the kind of skin that got sunburned easily, but now, Lucy noticed, he was redder than ever. "I never said thanks for the poem. I really liked it."

"That's okay." Lucy hesitated a moment. "You want to come in? You can watch Hobie and me eat pie à la mode."

"Okay. I might even find room for some myself."

When they were spooning up the last drops of vanilla, Lucy said, "Hobie's going for his final evaluation Saturday."

"So soon?" Cal's face caved in like the crust of the campers' pie. He crouched down and stroked Hobart's ears.

"Yeah." Lucy blinked her eyes furiously. She hated crying. She grabbed a dish towel and turned her back so she could give her eyes a quick swipe.

"Lu?" Cal said, before she'd turned back around. "How about giving Hobie a going-away present? A week where we devote ourselves entirely to doggy pursuits. You know, playing Frisbee, going to the park—and eating lots of ice cream."

Lucy flashed him a grateful smile. "Okay, sure." She thought of Emily Dickinson's poem, the one that began, "The Brain is wider than the Sky." For the next week she was going to burn every detail about Hobie into her memory. That way she could keep a little part of him forever.

"Hobie's got the only mouth I ever met that could eat ice cream faster than mine," Cal told Lucy as they strolled home from the park. "He had me beat by at least three minutes today."

Lucy shook her head. "You can't beat a dog at eating. Didn't you ever hear the expression 'to wolf down your food'? Eating quickly is in Hobie's genes. From the days when he had to grab his share faster than the other wild dogs or else starve to death."

"I bet Hobie would've hated living back then. Probably the closest cave dogs ever came to ice cream was snow cones."

Lucy smiled. Ahead of her on his leash, Hobart was prancing with his Frisbee in his mouth. Prancing! It was a word she'd never thought she'd be able to use to describe him. He'd become a different dog in the time he'd been living with her. Happy. Playful. Pride swelled like a balloon in her throat and kept her from speaking.

When they reached the next corner, Lucy could see Jeremy's yellow Toyota parked in her driveway. Like the yellow rose of Texas, she thought, chuckling to herself. Anna and Jeremy were sitting on the hood. When they saw Lucy and Cal, they waved.

"Looks like your sister and her boyfriend are catching some rays," Cal remarked. "Either that, or someone put Krazy Glue on the hood of that car."

"Want to come over and say hello? Jeremy's not so bad, you know."

"Can't. Swim practice is in half an hour. Got to get ready."

"Chicken!"

"You mean tuna. See you later."

"Bye. Try not to drown, Tuna."

Jeremy waved as Lucy came up the driveway. "Hey, Lucy, it looks like Hobart's permanently attached to that Frisbee."

"Almost," Lucy agreed. "I'm going to pack it up with his other things, so he can take it with him."

"I heard." Jeremy looked down at his hands. "I know how hard it's going to be to give him up."

Lucy shrugged. "Someone out there's waiting for him." Her eyes wandered down the street as if she could see that person now.

Jeremy followed her gaze, silently rubbing his chin back and forth across his knuckles. "Anna and I were wondering if you'd let us drive you and Hobie over to the Guiding Friends Center on Saturday morning?"

Lucy turned and met his eyes. "Okay. Thanks." She felt Anna's arm slide around her shoulders.

"Come on, Hobie," Jeremy said, jumping off the hood. "Let's us guys go play some Frisbee."

. . .

On Friday night, they had a farewell barbecue for Hobart. The guest list included Mr. and Mrs. Schaeffer and Zeus, Cal and his mother, Jeremy, Anna, Mrs. Rising, and Lucy. Mrs. Schaeffer came across the backyard carrying a little tree hung with rawhide chews and dog biscuits. It was supposed to be a centerpiece, but Hobart and Zeus demolished it before it ever made it to the picnic table.

After dinner, Anna and Jeremy left to see the movie they'd missed the night Jeremy had to mow the lawn. The adults went indoors for coffee and dessert. And Lucy and Cal stayed outside to grill marshmallows over the glowing coals. Lucy had just stuck a sugary pillow on a skewer, when her mother came back out of the house.

"Lucy, phone call! It's your father."

"Where is he?"

"Australia. Come on in."

Lucy watched her marshmallow catch fire. "What does he want?"

Her mother took a long, deep breath, as though she were gathering something more than air inside herself. "I don't know. To talk. Now hurry up or his phone bill is going to cost more than his airfare home." She turned and started toward the house.

"Go ahead, Lu. I'll finish cooking your marshmallow," Cal said.

Lucy stared into the hot coals. The marshmallow's powdery surface shriveled and blackened. After a few more seconds, it turned completely to ashes and dropped into the fire with an angry hissing sound. Lucy handed Cal her skewer and walked slowly to the house.

"Hello?"

"Lulu! I thought maybe you weren't coming."

"I'm here."

"Honey, I want you to know I'm not mad at you for not writing. Even if you're still mad at me."

"You're the one who left."

"I had to. I couldn't be happy at home, no matter how hard I tried. I thought you'd understand."

Your happiness! Lucy wanted to shout. *What about mine?* But she only asked, "Then why are you coming back now?"

There was a long pause at the other end of the line. He's not coming after all, Lucy thought. She didn't even feel angry. Just empty as a vacant house.

"Lucy, listen to me! I'm coming back because I miss you and Anna too much."

"No, you're not. You're coming back to get a divorce."

"That's not true. I mean, your mother and I are getting divorced, but that's not why I'm returning."

"Are you going to marry her?"

"You mean Sarah? No. She needs to live in Australia. I need to live where I can be close to you. I'm going to start looking for an apartment in the city as soon as I get home. With extra bedrooms for you and

Anna to stay in whenever you want to. One that allows pets."

"Don't bother," Lucy said. "Hobie's going back to Guiding Friends tomorrow."

"Your mother told me. I'll get you another puppy. If Mom doesn't want it around, you can keep it at my place."

Lucy squeezed her eyes shut tightly. She had the weird feeling she'd somehow become older than her father. "No, Dad. I need to feel that Hobie's gone for a while." She paused, waiting for the throbbing behind her eyes to stop. When she spoke again, her voice came out in a whisper. "I guess some things just have to hurt. It's how you know they matter."

"Lucy, I love you," her father said. His voice was thick and hoarse. "Will you come and stay at my hotel when I get in? Help me look for an apartment?"

"I don't know."

"I understand—you need time to think about it. I'll call you, okay?"

"Bye, Daddy."

21

Anna fiddled with the stations on the radio while Jeremy drove. In the backseat, Lucy sat perfectly still, holding a bag with Hobie's red Frisbee, his bandana, a last rawhide chew Mrs. Schaeffer had salvaged from the centerpiece, and a letter Lucy had written describing the dog's likes and dislikes. Beside her, Hobie sat up and poked his head out the window. He seemed to enjoy how the wind felt against his face.

"What's going to happen?" Jeremy asked. "Will you get to watch the evaluation?"

"No, they don't allow the raisers to stay. Brenda says it's too hard for some people to resist interfering. Sometimes they cheer their dogs on from the sidelines and distract all the others. Or else they argue with the judges if they think their dogs haven't been given a fair chance to perform."

"Will they tell you where he's going? I mean, if he passes the evaluation?" In the rearview mirror, Lucy could see creases around Jeremy's eyes and across his forehead.

"Yes. I'll be invited to his graduation from training school. His new owner will be there with him."

"That's good, I guess."

"Do you really think you should go to the gradua-tion?" Anna asked. "I'm not sure I could bear it."

"Brenda says seeing the dogs and their masters walk down the aisle together makes the whole experience worthwhile," Lucy told her. "Besides, I have to see for myself that he's happy. Not knowing would be worse."

Jeremy pulled up in front of the office. "Should we go in with you?"

"No. I want to do it myself." Lucy slipped out the door with Hobart following her. She thought he looked alert and dignified—like he was already the perfect guide dog.

Only a few moments passed before she was back, gripping the empty leash in her hand.

22

On Sunday morning, Lucy and Mrs. Rising decided to make blueberry muffins. Upstairs, Anna was still asleep. At first, their conversation centered around measuring cups and oven temperature—not at all, Lucy knew, like the private murmuring that went on between her mother and her sister. But while she was mixing flour and eggs together, Mrs. Rising said, "I guess you miss Hobie already."

Lucy gazed into the bowl and nodded. "Brenda said keeping busy is the best way to deal with it."

"She's right. It's the best way to deal with any loss."

Her mother's wistful tone made Lucy remember all the projects she'd tried to involve her in last winter, like the tie-dyeing and the tap dancing. She wished she'd been more agreeable about them. Maybe her mother had needed those distractions even more than she did. "Mom? Are you trying to keep busy now because of Mr. Stern being away?"

Mrs. Rising twisted her nose and lips off to the left. Finally she answered, "Not really. Rick's a nice man, but our relationship was just getting started. He was hardly part of my regular routine. We'll see what happens when he comes back."

"Oh."

"But I was hoping we could save a couple of muffins for Danielle. I know she misses her daddy a lot right now."

"Maybe we could take her to dinner at McDonald's one night after camp."

"What a nice idea! She's been staying with her grandmother. I'll call and arrange it later."

"Okay." Lucy was about to pour the batter into the muffin cups when the phone rang. She licked off a fingertip and picked up the receiver. "Hello?"

"Good morning, Lucy. This is Brenda. We finished evaluating the dogs last night and I'm calling to tell you the results."

Lucy's body stiffened the way Hobart's did when he was frightened. She could even feel the tiny hairs along her arms and the back of her neck stand up. Brenda's voice sounded distant and echoey, like she was calling to Lucy through a long, dark tunnel. For a moment, Lucy couldn't even speak.

"Lucy, are you there?"

Lucy hadn't realized she was holding her breath. She let it out in a big puff. "Did Hobie pass?"

"I'm afraid not."

Lucy had already made it across the pond—twice, in a way. She'd thought she'd been safe. But this time, she could feel the ice cracking under her feet. And she and Hobie were both slipping through. Only, it wasn't fair! It was she who'd failed, not him. Couldn't Brenda see that?

"Why not?" She wanted to sound angry, but her voice wouldn't cooperate. It came out more like a plea. A prayer. "Why not? He was the best dog in the class."

"Yes, he was—when you were with him. But without your encouragement, he just doesn't have enough confidence to face the daily challenges of negotiating the streets. It's a testament to the job you did with him that he was able to perform so well in class. Really, you were wonderful. And so is Hobart. But not without you."

Until now, Lucy had tried not to think about the evaluation. But she could no longer stop the pictures from flooding her mind. Hobie being ordered around by strangers. Being subjected to loud noises and confused by "surprises," like having an umbrella popped open in his face. She knew for the sake of their future owners, the dogs' courage had to be tested. It was a matter of life and death. But her heart felt like it was falling through space when she imagined Hobie searching for her among all the unfamiliar faces. She knew just how his ears would lie flat back and his tail would droop between his legs when he was commanded to do something scary. She could see his eyes becoming moist and mournful when he failed.

"What's going to happen to him?" Lucy whispered. She felt her mother slide an arm around her shoulders. She took the receiver off her ear and held it between their heads so they could both listen.

"We're hoping you'll agree to keep him. And that

you'll continue with Guiding Friends as a volunteer training aide. Hobie would make a great demonstration dog in the puppy program, don't you think?"

Lucy turned to look at Mrs. Rising. Her eyelashes were wet and shiny. "Yes," she told Brenda. "I know he'd be really good at it."

"So, do you think your mother will agree to the arrangement?"

Mrs. Rising squeezed her shoulder. "She thinks it's fine," Lucy said.

"Wonderful. While we've got Hobart here, we'll give him a physical to update his shots and stuff. You can pick him up this afternoon. Will that be okay?"

"Yes!" Suddenly Lucy remembered something. "Brenda—what about Comanche?"

"He passed the evaluation with flying colors. I've just finished telling David."

In her mind, Lucy saw Comanche with little rainbow-striped angel wings growing from his shoulders. He was flying around the church basement like a stunt pilot, doing flips and nosedives above the heads of the trainers. "That's great," she told Brenda. "Uh—do you have David's telephone number? I'd like to call and congratulate him."

"Sure. Hold on and I'll get it for you."

David answered on the first ring. "Hello?"

"Hi, it's Lucy. I just heard Comanche made it. I wanted to say congratulations."

"Thanks." David let out a long breath before he added, "What about Hobart?"

"He failed." A burning feeling at the back of her throat made it hard for Lucy to talk. "Brenda said without me, he just didn't have enough confidence."

David was silent for a moment. "Well, I still think he's a great dog."

"Yeah." Lucy remembered what she'd said to her father. *Some things just have to hurt.* It was true. If Hobie had passed the evaluation, if he was no longer going to be part of her life, that would have hurt, too. Even though she was sure she knew the answer, she asked, "How are you feeling?"

David cleared his throat, but his voice was still froggy. "Good—and bad. I'm trying to keep busy, like Brenda said. In the fall, I'm going to raise another pup."

"You are?"

"Yep. I like feeling as if I'm doing something for the world, even if it's just in a small way."

"I'll be going to classes in the fall, too! Brenda's asked me to work as a training aide with Hobie."

David's voice brightened. "Really? That's great! Then I guess I'll see you there."

"Yes. But if you feel like playing with a dog before then, you can come over and visit."

"Thanks, I'd like that. I think I may need to wait a while, though. You know what I mean?"

"As a matter of fact, I do."

. . .

When the muffins were in the oven, Lucy bounded up the stairs. She felt like she was flying, though not quite like Comanche with his rainbow wings. Her flight was more of a time trip. Like she was gliding over the past year, looking down at her life. She'd lost a lot of people she'd loved. And now it seemed she'd gotten them back in one way or another. Yet she wasn't sure if things had really changed at all—or if it was that she had.

Later, when Cal came back from swim practice, she would tell him the news about Hobie. But now, she sat down at her desk and turned on The Great Eye. Then she began writing a poem. Maybe she would send it to Mr. Frye. Or someday, she might show it to her father.

THE GREAT EYE
The Great Eye blinks and opens wide
it keeps my hopes and dreams inside
it hears the voice that no ear will
the one inside when I am still
The soul that is not good or bad
or right or wrong or bright or sad
but which at times is all those things
The Great Eye gives each aspect wings

The Great Eye blinks, the tear is shed
that's trapped inside my aching head
It gives release to thoughts that throb,

cares that burn, wishes that bob
like little boats that will not sink
The Great Eye blinks, the Great Eye blinks

The Great Eye blinks, the sky appears
vast, inviting, free of fears
I don my wings and pass right through
flying till I'm out of view
No longer bound by things that are
I soar to sun and moon and star
When I look back the world I see
is newly sweet, awaiting me